I0598378

Bitter Autumn

by

Loretta C. Rogers

This is a work of fiction. Names, characters, places, and incidents are either the product of the author's imagination or are used fictitiously, and any resemblance to actual persons living or dead, business establishments, events, or locales, is entirely coincidental.

Bitter Autumn

COPYRIGHT © 2020 by Loretta C. Rogers

All rights reserved. No part of this book may be used or reproduced in any manner whatsoever without written permission of the author or The Wild Rose Press, Inc. except in the case of brief quotations embodied in critical articles or reviews.
Contact Information: info@thewildrosepress.com

Cover Art by *Diana Carlile*

The Wild Rose Press, Inc.
PO Box 708
Adams Basin, NY 14410-0708
Visit us at www.thewildrosepress.com

Publishing History
First Cactus Rose Edition, 2020
Print ISBN 978-1-5092-3124-9
Digital ISBN 978-1-5092-3125-6

Published in the United States of America

She did not want to wake up. It was the large hands removing her wet clothing that startled a fearful gasp from her. She forced her eyes to open. A man hovered over her. He was hardly more than an ominous gray shadow inside a crude shelter, and she thought his eyes glowed with a feral light. In her delirium and thinking he was Levi High Eagle, she shrank back and had some difficulty breathing as she awaited her fate. Drawing up in a small, disconcerted knot, she waited to be punished.

The snow had seemingly spent its furor. Birdie was thoroughly depleted, both physically and mentally. Though she tried to remain alert, her eyelids sagged beneath the weight of her fatigue. She tried to lift her head, until a large hand pressed it down gently against a sturdy shoulder. Her brow found a warm niche for nestling, against a corded neck, and with a sigh, she gave up her futile attempts to remain conscious. If Levi High Eagle intended to kill her, he would have done so by now.

Darkness had fallen. Birdie roused briefly to a vague awareness that the snow had ended. A cold, blustery wind had sprung up. The frigid breezes evoked shivers. Birdie reached to tighten her coat closer to her body, only to realize that she wore strange clothing. A hairy arm drew her snug against a bare chest. She found no energy to resist but nestled closer to soak up the warmth. As she drifted off to sleep again, she was reminded that once again she had been captured and wondered distantly if she would ever find a safe haven.

Praise for Loretta C. Rogers and...

MURDER IN THE MIST: "Lots of suspense, great characters, and some romance tossed in for good measure."

~*Coffee Time Romance*

BANNON'S BRIDES: "I was so taken with the story and characters I read this book in one day."

~*Reading for the Love of Books*

THE WITCHING MOON: "Part paranormal, part western, and part suspense romance. 100 percent enjoyable."

~*A Reader*

SHADOWED REUNION: "Action packed with a riveting blend of romance and suspense."

~*Book Lover*

WHEN COMES FOREVER: "A visual and engaging Historical with romance and suspense."

~*Netgalley*

MURDER IN THE MIST: "Fast paced suspense is a nail biter!!"

~*Audible Audio*

**Also available from The Wild Rose Press
books by Loretta C. Rogers**

Isabelle and the Outlaw
McKenna's Woman
Bannon's Brides
Forbidden Son
Lady Adel's Captain
Cloud Woman's Spirit
Murder in the Mist
Shadowed Reunion
Taming the Lyon
Fate Comes Softly
When Comes Forever

CAST OF CHARACTERS

Sisters by Circumstance
Birdie Mae Dix—kidnapped at age five; rescued at age twenty-three
Esther Bullard—kidnapped at age twenty-five; rescued at age forty-five
Ja'meena Picket—kidnapped at age forty-two; rescued at age forty-six

The Men Who Loved Them
Captain Ford Thackery—forfeited wealth for a military career; age thirty-six
Sergeant Ansel Miller—grizzled and war-weary; age fifty
Sergeant Isaiah Bohanan—a buffalo soldier; age fifty

The Insane
Emmaline Borski—attacks without provocation
Lucy Nelson—giggles at everything
Minnie Sudbury—bites as her defense
Clara Butler—spits on people
Nancy Cartwright—mute
Patricia Sherman—converses with imaginary people

Fort Ellis
Colonel Myles Culpepper—fort commander
Nora Culpepper—champions the captive women
Dr. Jethro Pope—fort doctor
Elmira Ledbetter—fort gossip
Army scout Levi High Eagle—Pawnee aka Mud Pony
Army scout Sam Two Feather—Kootenai tribe

Chapter One

Montana 1877

Woman with Iron Fist huddled with the small group of old women, old men, and children. Beneath the threadbare blanket draped around her frail body, she held her six-year-old son's hand. His shivers vibrated against her hip. He did not whimper from the cold or from the hunger she knew gnawed at his belly. She was weary. They were all weary, the old, the sick, the young. Many had died along the trail. All were frightened. And now, once again, she was a captive.

A man's voice interrupted her meandering thoughts. The words though familiar were also foreign. She wondered why he yelled at them. Was he angry? Did he think they were deaf?

"Any of you heathens speak English?"

English?

She searched her mind. Yes, a long time ago, she had spoken such words, and they had flowed from her tongue. Vague memories of another time flooded her mind and bruised her heart. It had been so long. How long? Many moons, and now the words of her white mother's tongue were as elusive as smoke.

The fleeting image of a woman with fiery red hair and eyes filled with laughter appeared within her imagination. It was as if she could hear the woman calling, *Birdie...Birdie.*

A flutter of wind tugged at the blanket, heightening her icy discomfort. Surely it was the wind that filled her ears with playful tricks.

Her eyes downcast, Woman with Iron Fist pulled the blanket tighter to hide her face. She clamped her teeth to the insides of her cheeks to squelch the desire to speak. Uncertainty on how many years had passed since she had uttered a single understandable English word caused her to bite harder until the tang of blood tainted her tongue. The few times she recalled speaking the words of her mother had always brought harsh, often brutal punishment.

The man shouted, "Eng-lish. Any of you ignoramuses speak Eng…lish?"

When no one responded, he shrugged and pivoted to walk away.

The child hugged tight against her leg. His shivers grew more violent and his fever seared through her thin dress. The rattle in his chest meant his sickness was getting worse. She had to save her son. She berated her mind for failing to remember the language of the woman with hair the color of a setting sun. Was this woman the mother she could no longer remember? The questions caused her head to ache.

Hugging her son close, she pushed through the group. "B-bur-dee." The word rose painfully from her throat. Her vocal cords constricted. She spoke louder. "Bur-dee."

The man in the blue coat whirled about. "Who said that?"

Fear of cruel punishment held her at bay. Concern for her starving son forced her forward. She pointed to her chest. "Bur-dee. Me."

His eyes widened as he leaned in for a closer look. "Good gawd almighty." He garnered another look. "Cap'n Thackery, you better come a-runnin'." His voice rose over the crunching snow as he trotted toward his commanding officer. "Cap'n! Cap'n Thackery, you ain't gonna believe this."

Captain Ford Thackery slapped his gloved hands together as if trying to ward off the chill. "Get these people moving, Sergeant Major. I'm cold, and wet, and hungry. I can only imagine how these poor devils feel. Let's get 'em back to the fort for processing."

"But, Cap'n…"

"Now! Sergeant Major Miller. That's an order."

"Beggin' pardon, sir, but we got us a white woman."

"Whi…white woman…where? Are you sure?"

"I'm fair certain Ind'ans don't have green eyes, sir. I believe she was trying to say her name, though I can't be for certain. Sounded like—Birdie."

Thackery removed his hat and shoved a gloved hand through his hair, mussing it, and uttering an exasperated sigh. "Show me."

Miller saluted. "Yessir. Right this way."

Powdery snow crunched under the men's boots until they stood in front of the small group that huddled together.

Sergeant Major Miller pointed. "You there, with the green eyes, step forward."

She remained still, wide-eyed, throat painfully tight, afraid to look away from the tall, broad-shouldered man, an enemy of her people. She shifted her gaze to the short, stout man with the raspy voice.

"That 'un there, Cap'n." Miller continued to point.

Uncertain she had understood the raspy-voiced man's words, she stood her ground.

The small throng parted as the captain stepped forward, leaving her exposed. "I'm Captain Ford Thackery, ma'am. What is your name?" He spoke softly, and slowly.

His gaze pierced her. She forced herself to stand perfectly still. Blue, she saw. His eyes were blue, as dark as possible without being black.

Beneath the brim of his black hat, his eyes remained steady on hers. "Are there others like you, Miss—?"

She felt a foolish, almost overwhelming urge to fling herself into the captain's arms and sob against his chest. She was a grown woman, not a child, and besides, such show of private emotions, especially to the enemy, would bring punishment.

She knew punishment. Unforgiving and painfully cruel, it had often had her praying for death to take her.

She remained wide-eyed, throat painfully tight, afraid to look away lest this man disappear like a dream, leaving her befuddled. The words came harsh and raw to her throat as she met his eyes. "Bur-dee."

His smile spoke kindness when he said, "Birdie? What is your last name?"

She stared at him in confusion. Last name? Indians had but one name. If she had another name, it had disappeared from her remembrance. She needed to think on this.

Pointing to his chest, he said, "Thackery. My last name is Thackery."

She pointed to him and repeated. "Thack-ry." And

then she pointed to herself and said, "Bur-dee."

"Never mind. We'll work on the names later." He enunciated each word as if to make sure she understood. "Are their others like you?"

She glanced around and shifted a little. "Others?"

Snow fell, thick and fast, and the wind grew bitter. Long shadows crept across the land. A damp chill iced Ford to the bone. He took a long look around him, a long look at the bedraggled group his Pawnee scout had accidentally come across while searching for Chief Joseph's band.

"Levi High Eagle, who are these people?"

The scout growled his disgust. "Some Nez Perce. Others slaves, maybe. Old and useless. Cannot travel fast. They were left behind to die." The scout jacked the rifle against his shoulder. "They are worthless."

Thackery swung his arm under the rifle barrel, knocking it upward. "Pull that trigger and I'll stand you in front of a firing squad." Hot anger sped through the captain, and he forgot his own freezing misery. "Get out of my sight, High Eagle. Go see if you can scour up some game. We'll need extra meat for tonight."

Thackery settled his gaze on the woman. She was especially tall, and reed thin. He suspected that if he were to snatch away the blanket she hugged so tightly to her body, he'd find mere skin and bones. Yet there was an air of dignity about her, and a quiet strength. A muscle clamped briefly in her jaw, and he noted the silent desperation in her eyes.

Ford's heart slammed against his backbone. In his initial surprise at discovering a white woman among savages, he'd not noticed the bulge at her side. She was hiding something. His temper flared. All Indians were the enemy, even the so-called tame ones. Captive or not, she was with them. This made her the enemy, too. "What're you hiding under the blanket—a weapon?"

Only the horses, swishing their tails and snorting and blowing against the cold, and the low grumbles riffling among the troopers disturbed the silence. He noted the weariness in the captives' eyes and the solemn droop of their shoulders. These people were near-starved, and scared to death. There was no wailing, no begging, as they awaited their fate.

With the swiftness of a rattler, Captain Ford Thackery clamped down on Birdie's arm and jerked her with such force that she fell to her knees.

The little boy tumbled from the blanket's meager warmth to land face down in the snow. Before he could react to the sight of a child, Birdie sprang to her feet, balled her fist, and struck Thackery on the chin with such force the blow staggered him backward.

A yodeling cheer went up amongst the captives. Voices in unison shouted, *"Ah-ho, Ah-ho, Wikhókalaka Mas'ikčekA Napómus!"*

Thackery brushed aside Sergeant Miller's efforts to keep him from falling. The heat from Thackery's face fanned his anger and embarrassment at being cold-cocked by a mere slip of a woman. Pride kept him from rubbing his chin. He shouted, "Levi High Eagle, front and center!"

The Pawnee scout dropped the reins to his horse and raced forward. Thackery commanded, "What are they saying?"

High Eagle sneered, "The people say, 'Yes, yes, Woman with Iron Fist.'"

She sensed the captain's disquiet as the scout

looked her up and down, his lascivious gaze taking in every inch of her disheveled appearance.

Without warning, Birdie flew at the Pawnee scout, venom in her snarls, murder in her eyes, hands curled into claws. Before she could do damage to the man's face, Thackery wrapped his arm around her waist and swung her to the ground. She came up spitting and snarling, and speaking a language only the people and the Pawnee understood.

She sprang to her feet, and in doing so scooped the wide-eyed little boy into her arms. She continued to point an accusing finger at the Pawnee, angry words spewing like hot lava from her mouth.

Thackery demanded, "What's she saying, High Eagle?"

The Pawnee gripped the hilt of his knife and backed away, shaking his head.

"Damn it, scout, I've issued you an order. I'll not ask again. What is she saying?"

Malice laced the scout's voice. "She say Pawnee murdering, dung-eating dogs." High Eagle swept the knife from his scabbard. "I cut out her tongue."

"Stand down, scout! That's an order." Thackery barred the Pawnee's way.

Thackery drew a breath when he frowned at the red-haired woman as she held the boy of about six. The blanket fell away from her body and floated across his boots in a damp heap. An immediate tightness filled his chest. He was certain that under all that filth was an exceptional beauty. A strange feeling came over him, a sensation he hadn't experienced in what seemed a lifetime, a sensation that filled him with an inexplicable desire to press her body against his. This rankled him.

7

The emaciated child still in her arms, Birdie marched forward, hawked a wad and spat it in the Pawnee's face. The people behind her laughed and pointed as the drool slid down Levi High Eagle's cheek. And they chanted, "Yes, yes, Woman with Iron Fist."

High Eagle's hand snaked out and grabbed Birdie by the throat. "Comanche whore. You die."

Thackery's eyes narrowed dangerously. "Sergeant Major Miller, take his weapons and assign Trooper Hayes to keep an eye on him."

With quick efficiency, the sergeant disarmed the scout.

Thackery glared at High Eagle. "If you go near the woman or any of these people, I'll order you shot on the spot."

Thackery's voice sharpened, "Sergeant Major?"

"Sir?"

"Do we have enough rations to feed these people?"

Miller scratched his chin. "Reckon barely, Cap'n. Want me to send Sam Two Feathers out to fetch in whatever game he can find?"

"Do it."

The burly officer spun sharply on his heel to carry out the orders, but the captain called him back. "One moment, Sergeant Major. There are still a couple of hours of daylight. As we have no wagons, instruct the troopers to assist the women and children onto their mounts. Any old men too frail to walk will ride double. The troopers are to lead the horses."

The sergeant major saluted. "Yessir."

"Also," Thackery continued, "pick two of your best riders. Make sure they have fresh mounts. They are to ride like their shirttails are on fire to the fort with a message to the colonel that we need three wagons, and provisions for two nights. Instruct them to inform the colonel that we will arrive with approximately thirty captives who volunteered their surrender."

Sergeant Major Miller again saluted his understanding and hastened to carry out his orders.

Thackery moistened his wind-dried lips. He turned his gaze toward Birdie. "Where is the boy's father?" He nodded toward the child at her side.

She had reached down to retrieve the threadbare blanket and had wrapped it around her shoulders and the boy in her arms. Silent, she stared at Thackery.

He repeated his question. "The boy's father—is he alive?"

She simply shrugged her shoulders.

"So be it. Follow me." Unsure if she had understood him, Thackery motioned for Birdie to follow him.

When she didn't move, he reached out to touch the jagged scar that tracked across her cheek and down the side of her neck. She shuddered as she drew to her full height. His eyes captured hers, and they reminded him of ocean green. How long had it been since he'd visited his grandparents and Cape Cod? He chastised himself. A hint of bewilderment flashed over her face, as if she, too, felt the strange sensation that passed between them. He snatched his hand away. What magic spell had this woman cast over him? It had been more years than he could remember since he'd thought of home.

Chapter Two

When the captain offered to carry the boy, Birdie batted his hand away.

"He's heavy. I'm only trying to help."

She hugged the child closer and sternly shook her head.

"Have it your way." He motioned for her to follow.

She trailed behind the captain. After several failed attempts at making her understand his requests, Thackery ordered Levi High Eagle front and center. "Whatever malice you hold toward this woman, keep it contained. Ask if there are more white women in this bunch."

The scout's eyes seemed to crackle with loathing as he asked Birdie if there were others like her.

She answered in Pawnee and pointed out women like herself.

Six were white; the others were Indian from other tribes. All were captives.

Some appeared broken in spirit, and all were emaciated.

Thackery walked among them. To himself he uttered, "My God."

It was impossible to gauge their ages. They were diseased and sick. Some keened their misery and hugged themselves while rocking back and forth. A few appeared mentally unhinged. Birdie, herself, feared she would never be normal again. Never trust. And worse, she was afraid of what fates awaited her.

Horses stood single file while troopers assisted those too frail to pull themselves into the saddles. Sergeant Miller escorted Birdie and her son to a broad-chested bay. "I'll hold the young'un whilst you climb aboard."

Birdie shook her head to indicate her refusal to get on the horse. Instead, she lifted her son onto the saddle. Then she raised her voice and called out as she pointed to a woman. The only word Sergeant Miller thought he understood was, "Ess-er."

A woman with brown hair streaked with silver strands, her eyes downcast, shoulders bent in servitude, trudged forward. She and Birdie exchanged words. The woman dared a look at the sergeant. Her eyes filled with fearful hope, she pointed to her chest. "Ess-er." Then her bent posture relaxed and with clarity, she said, "Esther."

Sergeant Miller crossed himself. "Mother be sainted. Another one."

Esther turned to lift her foot into the stirrup. Her knees went out from under her. In one swift motion, Sergeant Miller caught her by the waist and his strong arms hoisted her into the saddle. She offered him a weak smile, then wrapped her blanket around the little boy now slumped over the saddle horn.

Birdie and the woman exchanged more words. The woman shrugged her shoulders and shook her head.

In a bold movement, Birdie tugged at the sergeant's sleeve. She pointed to her son and spoke more words.

He spread his gloved hands wide. "I'm sorry as can

11

be, ma'am, but I just don't understand what yer sayin'. Hold on while I get High Eagle."

At the scout's name, Birdie scowled and shook her head in an obvious refusal. She pointed to her son, then to the sergeant, and then toward where the captain sat mounted on a tall red horse.

Before Miller could react further, Captain Thackery called out, "Front and center, Sergeant Major. Let's get these people moving."

Miller hesitated. "Sorry, ma'am." He hastened to where a trooper held a horse. He gathered the reins and swung into the saddle. He gigged the animal to the front of the line, raised his hand, and ordered, "Single file and at a walk."

When at last the horse in front of her moved, she looked at the woman called Esther and spoke. Esther removed the blanket from the child and handed it to Birdie. She gathered the little boy beneath her own threadbare blanket and then spoke in the language of the Nez Perce. "Soon you will sing your song of grief."

Birdie grabbed the stirrup to steady herself as she walked alongside the horse. She blinked away a fluttering snowflake that landed on her eyelash. "He is all that I have. Maybe there is a medicine man in the white man's camp. Maybe he make strong potion for my son."

"Ashkii's death rattles are strong against my chest. I feel in my spirit that the Great Father is calling his name. If the boy answers, do not be sad. The happy hunting grounds are a far better place for a boy to grow into a strong warrior."

"No! He is all I have."

"It has been many moons since I lived with the one

called husband. In many ways he was more cruel than the Sioux and the Arapaho. If Ashkii lives, he will be weak from this sickness in his lungs. He will never have the strength of a warrior. Do you wish for him to be the camp's lackey?"

"Saaaa…you speak true, Ess-er." Though the words stung Birdie's heart, she took comfort that her son would never know the lash across his back; he would never be treated as less than a dog; never more would he cry out in his sleep when his stomach cramped from hunger; and he would be a slave to no man, red or white. She looked upward at gunmetal gray clouds billowing in the darkening sky and whispered, "Great Father…I give you my son."

Briefly the clouds parted and rays of sun reached out like beckoning fingers. A keening wind kicked up. Horses snorted and troopers held tight to the prancing animals' reins. As quickly as it appeared the sun disappeared, and the wind died, and Birdie knew the Great Father had heard her prayer. It would be soon. Very soon.

She trudged next to the gelding. Soaked to the skin and thoroughly downcast, she blinked and tried to force back the tears that moistened her cheeks.

****

In the dying day, Captain Thackery halted the column and issued an order to make camp. An hour later, Levi High Eagle and Trooper Hayes rode through the encampment, a deer carcass tied behind High Eagle's saddle and a few snowshoe rabbits dangling from Private Hayes' saddle horn.

Several troopers had gathered enough wood to build three blazing fires in addition to a smaller cook fire. By the time night had flung its tapestry of stars across the sky, the air was redolent with smells of cooking meat. The aroma blended with the clean fresh fragrance of the snowy expanse and set Birdie's stomach growling with hunger. Like the other captives, she sat close to the flickering flames. While the warmth gradually relieved her feet and hands of the cold, the heat from her son's fever scorched her breasts. She leaned close to his face. His shallow breathing barely feathered her cheek.

Minute after agonizing minute sloughed past as she rocked back and forth crooning to her son. His wheezing grew worse. She did not know when she surrendered to sleep. She did not know when Ashkii drew his last breath. She jerked alert when someone touched her shoulder and spoke her name.

"Ma'am...Birdie?" Captain Thackery squatted beside her with a cup of steaming liquid in one hand and a plate of venison and fried bread in the other.

Her stomach squeezed and hunger gnawed at her. She shifted to ease her discomfort. The blanket around her shoulders parted, and a little limp arm fell through the opening. She pushed the wrap farther and stared at the closed eyes of her son, the peacefulness on his face, and then into the flint blue eyes of the captain holding forth a plate of food. All thoughts of hunger vanished.

She clutched the lifeless body to her chest. It seemed that no night birds chirped, no coyotes yodeled. Even the wind was silent. No sound could be heard but the quiet swish of the horses' tails. And even as the icy talons of alarm and sorrow clawed at her heart, from deep within her indomitable spirit, her voice came, desolate, as she gazed at Thackery through tear-laced lashes. "My son sleeps with the stars now." She tried to stand on legs that wobbled.

Thackery set the food aside as he hastened to keep Birdie from falling. For a moment she thought she saw pity in his eyes. He said, quietly, "I don't know what you're saying, but I know death when I see it. Sorry as I can be." He yelled, "Sergeant Major Miller, Sam Two Feathers, on the double."

Sam Two Feathers heaved a breath as he sprinted forward and saluted the captain. "Sir?"

"This woman's child has succumbed to a fever. Tell her we are sorry for her loss and that we will help her bury him in the white man's way."

The scout made several attempts to make Birdie understand. When she made no response, he shrugged his shoulders. "I have tried Pawnee, Sioux, and even the language of my Kootenai people, and Nez Perce. She no speak, she no blink. I think maybe this woman is daft."

The woman named Esther rose to place her hands around Birdie's shoulders. Her voice soft and filled with compassion, she reached for the child.

Birdie's lips curled back in a predatory snarl, like a lioness protecting her cub; her hair had come undone and spilled down in a burnished cascade over her shoulders. Her face, stained with soot and layers of grime, radiated an aura of fury, and then, "AAAAAAAAHeeeeeeyaaaa!" her scream rose to a shrill peak.

"Oh, me sainted mother." Sergeant Miller crossed himself as he stumbled backward at the inhuman shriek.

Birdie fled the circle of people, with Esther, Captain Thackery, Sergeant Miller, and the Kootenai scout giving chase until Birdie staggered and fell to her knees, gasping for breath. She waited, her heart pounding in her chest, while her senses gradually cleared.

Esther knelt in the snow and said something to her. Birdie glanced at the woman's solemn face. She exhaled softly and nodded.

Sam Two Feathers translated Birdie's sing-song words. "Ashkii means *boy*. My son did not live long enough to go on a vision quest to earn his warrior name."

She stood quiet for such a length of time that it seemed she had drifted to a faraway place before she spoke again. "A long time ago, more than I can count on my fingers, I had a dream of a little boy with hair the color of fire and skin white like snow. His name was Toe…mee. He was not of the People as I am not of the People. Ashkii and Toe-mee are no more. Killer of Bears is dead, too. I did not cry for the man who planted his seed in me. I did not sing his mourning song. He was as cruel as his name."

Sam Two Feathers continued to translate. Still clutching the child to her chest, it seemed an effort for her to speak. She looked into Ford Thackery's blue eyes. In the weighted silence that followed, it struck her that behind his sympathetic smile was a virile man with a steely core. Looking away, she let out a taut sigh. "Leave me while I mourn my son."

Her back rigid, she walked into the night, trying not to think of tomorrow, trying not to be afraid of the future.

****

Ford settled in the blanket, his head resting against

his saddle. His mind meandered from one thought to another—what to do about the dwindling food supplies, how many more deaths before arriving at Fort Ellis, and a tangle of thoughts over Woman with Iron Fist…Birdie.

"Cap'n?" The sergeant's intruding voice prickled him.

Ford sat up. "Trouble, Sergeant?"

"No, sir." Sergeant Miller stood splay-legged. "Tonight's one of those nights when I'd like us to dispense with the formalities and talk like the friends we are. That is, if you don't mind."

Ford patted the ground beside him. "What's on your mind, Ansel?"

Sergeant Ansel Miller lowered to his haunches. "You ever think about retiring from this man's army?"

"A time or two. You?"

"I'm coming up on my fiftieth birthday, and in a few months I'll have given nigh on thirty-two years to the service. I've fought in more campaigns than I care to think about, and truth be told, I'm just plain weary."

Ford scooted to a sitting position. "I've put in eighteen. I could retire in two years. The Army's all I know. What would you do with yourself, Ansel?"

"I could ask you the same thing. What were you before the Army, Ford? I mean, you went to West Point, so your family must've done something other than farm. Politics, maybe?"

Ford chuckled. "As a matter of fact, my father had the largest and best apple orchard in upstate New York, and he did dabble in politics. My grandfather owned a fleet of fishing boats, so when we weren't picking apples, my two brothers and I looked forward to spending time with my grandparents on Cape Cod." He pondered a moment. "I think farming would suit me right fine, Ansel. And you?"

"Well I'll be hornswoggled, a country gentleman farmer. That's just what I'd had in mind. Not that I'd be much of a gentleman farmer." He loosed a low guffaw. "More like a hardworking, sweat-drenched farmer. You think I'm too old to produce a young 'un or two?"

"Ansel, I think you can do anything you set your mind to."

Ansel scratched under his chin and cleared his throat. "Um, the woman, Esther, you think she'd go for an ole geezer like me?"

Ford smiled. So he wasn't the only one with a woman invading his thoughts. He tried to keep his comment neutral. "Only she and the other women know the horrors and hardships they've endured. I expect that in time, with a gentle way, and patience, and understanding, she or any of the women might adjust to a different way of living."

Ansel Miller snorted. "Well, you sure pussy-footed around that 'un. I know all of what you said. It's just that I ain't much to look at, with this paunch belly and bandy legs, and a balding spot under my cap. And Esther…Miss Esther—I suspect onct she was a refined lady."

When Ford didn't comment, Miller stood. He brushed snow off his backside. "Aw, forget it. Me and my crazy notions, that's all."

"Ansel?" Ford called him back. "It's not a crazy notion. You'd make any woman a fine husband. The thing is with Birdie, Esther, and the demented women, you have to expect the unexpected. If pursuing Esther is your aim, then good luck to you both. You don't need my blessing or anyone else's."

Ansel nodded. "Tomorrow we'll go back to being officers, respecting our ranks. For tonight, I'm 'bliged for the friendly conversation."

Ford lay back with his hands tucked beneath his head. Gazing at the stars, he rehashed the conversation. His thoughts drifted to the lines of Birdie's throat, her jaw, and how her lips reminded him of a puckered heart. Lips meant for kissing. He inhaled deeply as if conjuring how she might smell after lingering in a tub filled with lilac-scented bubble soap. His body responded to how he'd love to show her all his gentleness, his hands exploring the curves of her slender body, until she quivered with wanting.

A wolf howled in the darkness, interrupting the thumping of Ford's manhood. Damn! He'd been without a woman too long. He felt the night close around him as he shifted to gaze at the campfire. Its flickering flames danced like two people entwined into one. He drifted to sleep with the image of a flame-haired, green-eyed beauty in his arms.

Chapter Three

A canopy of mist hovered over the slow-moving column of horses, soldiers, and weary captives. Here along the Gallatin forest, warmth from the day was fleeting. Temperatures threatened to turn colder.

In the waning light, Sergeant Miller pulled his horse abreast of Ford Thackery's. Miller grumbled, his breath clouding the air, "We've had a half-night and four full days of slow going, Cap'n. I checked with Corporal Lafferty over to the mess wagon. He says supplies are mighty thin. Not even enough flour to scrape up a pan of biscuits, much less enough beans to fill a pot. Seasoning meat and salt depleted. With six new souls gone to meet their maker, I'm a-feared more of these poor devils ain't gonna make it to the fort if'n Tibbets and Smith don't get back soon. I'm telling you, Cap'n, I feel plumb sorry for all of 'em. 'Specially Miss Birdie. She ain't et enough to keep a sparrow alive since her poor little 'un died. Why, my own stomach feels like it's grown to my backbone. I can only imagine how she feels, her and Miss Esther. Worse, High Eagle and Two Feathers ain't found nary a sign of game. Not even a skunk or a porcupine."

"Stow it, Sergeant. Complaining won't make the situation any better. If our riders don't show up by tomorrow morning, then we can assume..." He stood in his stirrups. "Hand me your glass."

Sergeant Miller quickly shoved a pair of binoculars toward his captain. "Sweet mother, I sure hope…hot damn…it's them, Cap'n. I can see 'em from here. Tibbets and Smith and two…no…three wagons, and a string of fresh horses."

"Halt the column, Sergeant. We'll camp here for the night. Have the scouts pass the word along the line so the people will know what's happening."

Thackery released a measured breath of relief. With no available game, killing horses as a last resort for meat did not sit well with him. "Sergeant, as soon as the wagons arrive, instruct the men to distribute blankets and a ration of food that does not need preparation. Have Corporal Lafferty prepare the biggest pot of stew he and his assistant can make, post haste, and coffee. Enough to feed every last one of us."

Sergeant Miller suppressed a happy smile when he snapped off a salute. "Yessir." His grin was a little wider as he turned his horse and galloped toward the mess wagon.

Horses were unsaddled and tethered. Feed bags of fresh oats were draped over the horses' heads.

New blankets were distributed, along with two slices of bread, beef jerky, dried apples, and opened cans of milk for the remaining few children. Birdie and Esther sat with the other women.

"I think this is the most luxurious meal I have ever eaten. Excepting maybe…" Birdie's voice hitched.

Esther chewed thoughtfully on a piece of jerky. "Except for what, Woman with Iron Fist?"

"I don't know. It's like sometimes I have a remembrance of the other time, before the Pawnee." In exasperation, she shook her head. "Es-ser, do you remember your other life before you were taken?"

"Saaa...mostly I have forgotten. Now that we travel to the white man's fort, memories invade my sleep."

"Why have you no children?"

Esther answered without enthusiasm. "It was not ordained for me to bear young ones. In many ways I am grateful."

Birdie answered in a tearful voice. "Saaa...my arms are heavy with emptiness." Her energy spent, she did not speak for a long while. "Do you wish to return to your other life?"

Esther gave Birdie a bland look. "Ah-ho...not to the one called husband." She wrinkled her forehead as if trying to remember. "It was a long time ago, when I was young. He was a cruel man named Ornie Bullard, part-time preacher, full-time alcoholic. For a long time after I was taken I used to pray for the cavalry to rescue me. I lay awake night after night and listened for the clank of sabers, for the sound of shod hooves." She made an abrupt swatting motion with her hand. "I do not wish to remember the days with Bullard or the days that followed after my capture. No more talk."

"One more question, Es-ser, please. Do you remember Eng-lish?"

"Why do you ask?"

"At this fort where we travel, do you trust Levi High Eagle or Sam Two Feathers to speak truth for us?"

"I need to think on this." Esther clutched the blanket closer to her face.

An hour of silence, an hour to think, to listen to her heartbeats, an hour for the mind to conjure up long nightmares out of the misshapen shadows of trees that appeared as vaporous ghosts. Birdie leaned her forehead against her knees and silently grieved.

Levi High Eagle called out in Nez Perce, "Line up, you sons of whores. Gorge your bellies on the white man's food, for tomorrow they may line you up and shoot you like the dogs you are."

Birdie scooted closer to Esther and whispered, "We have lived long with the People, but our skin and hair is different. Do you still need to think about trusting a Pawnee and a Kootenai to speak for us?"

****

The three wagons were filled with all that remained of the original thirty-five captives. Birdie, Esther, six white women of undeterminable age whose minds were broken, a woman whose tongue had been split so she could no longer speak, seven Mexican women, and five mixed-blooded children—three girls and two boys— were separated from the others and loaded together. Birdie tried to drive the worry from her mind.

Feeling a soft nudge against her ribs, she cast a questioning glance toward Esther, who nodded in the direction of the formidable image of Captain Thackery riding toward their wagon. She shivered as a chilly draft wafted beneath her thin deer-hide skirt. She stifled a sneeze with a slender finger.

Next to the high-sided wagon, Ford halted his gelding, relaxed in the saddle, and tipped his hat. "Morning, ladies. The journey won't be as long as it has been. Wish I could offer you more comfort."

He looked down at Birdie with a faint smile, his eyes a smoldering blue. She stared him, a blush heating her cheeks. Was he the enemy, as Levi High Eagle had proclaimed? Could this man with silver tips lining his hair be trusted? With renewed interest, as if seeing Ford for the first time, not as a foe but as a gift from the Great Father above, as someone who had given her food and a new blanket and had not demanded any sexual favors as payment.

She touched her lips, then motioned with her hands that she did not understand his words. "Never mind. I'll teach you," he said, as he gigged his horse forward.

She turned to watch him as he cantered to the head of the column. The one called sergeant joined him. Thackery raised his hand and motioned forward, while the sergeant, in his deep resonant voice called, "Move 'em out."

An eternity seemed to pass before the soldier on the board seat slapped the reins and the team finally drew the wagon onward, its iron-rimmed wheels crunching in the snow.

A little girl with lice-infested brown hair asked, "Are they taking me to my mommy?"

A Mexican woman's words were harsh as she pinched the child.

No one else spoke.

The wagons bumped and jostled along the rough route. Certain her body was bruised from head to toe, Birdie was grateful for the new blanket and the meager heat generated from the closely huddled bodies. No matter how uncomfortable, riding was a relief from trudging through the snow. Periodic stops were made for nooning and to allow the horses to rest. Bread and jerky became the staple until stopping for the night. Birdie relished the plates of beans, more bread, and coffee served as supper. Her stomach no longer gnawed with hunger.

At nightfall the tenth day, the cramped wagons approached the fort that loomed like a dark phantom in the middle of a bleak and snow-covered plain. It was a desolate place, grim, and foreboding.

Excited voices from the soldiers roused Birdie and the other women from their sleep. One of the women suffering from prairie fever rose up to peer over the high-sided wagon. Beset with hysterical giggles, she shirked off her blanket and grabbed the driver, spewing words of gibberish from her broken mind.

Birdie and Esther gripped her around the waist and pulled her down to the bed of the wagon. Cradling her like a child, Esther said, "Poor lost soul. It would have been better if the Great Father had claimed her before the madness took her."

"What will become of her and the other mad ones?" Birdie eyed Esther in an honest gaze.

Her only answer was a shrug. Birdie rose to her knees to peer at the looming structure.

Captain Thackery raised his hand and called a halt to the caravan. He spoke loudly to two men holding rifles. Birdie watched as the massive wooden gates opened wide. Horses were clucked and once again the wagons moved forward.

A dog barked until a voice shouted for it to shut up. The boardwalks were lined with the fort's inhabitants. The convoy made for a curious audience as it rattled into the yard of Fort Ellis.

Birdie whispered, "I feel as if we have ridden straight into the heart of a hornet's nest. Look at how they stare at us." She beseeched Esther, "Please, oh, please, try to remember Eng-lish."

"Saaa...brain hurts from the effort. I can recall a

few words, but try as I might I cannot form a complete sentence in my mind. For now, perhaps, it is wise to remain silent and listen."

"Ah-ho. Especially to the twisted words of the Pawnee dog. I thought the Kootenai were friends of the Nez Perce. It seems Sam Two Feathers speaks with forked tongue also. For what reason, I do not know."

Esther nodded her agreement. "I think we can trust the one known as Mil-ler. He has honest eyes."

In the middle of the yard, Captain Thackery lifted his hand and called a halt to the caravan. He dismounted and handed the reins to someone called Private. Struggling to understand his words, Birdie listened to Thackery's orders. Instinctively she knew that to survive in her new world, she must relearn the tongue of her mother's people.

Birdie and Esther held hands as they watched an older man stride out to meet Thackery. The two men exchanged salutes, then shook hands. There was a great deal of pointing at buildings, gesturing toward the wagons, and loud voices that sounded angry.

"Arrogant sons of devils." A ghost of a vicious smile tugged at the Pawnee scout's lips.

She gasped at High Eagle's low-spoken malicious words. She had been so engrossed in watching Thackery and the other man she had not heard the Pawnee scout pull his horse next to the wagon. She clutched Esther's hand even tighter.

In a moment, the older man spun on his heel to walk toward a building where he reentered a brightly lit room. After conversing with Sergeant Miller, Captain Thackery hastened across the yard and up the steps. He knocked and then entered the same room.

Chapter Four

At Sergeant Major Miller's instructions, High Eagle called out for the captives to stay in the wagons until told to disembark, and then they were to line up single file and follow Sam Two Feathers. The Pawnee scout stood high in the stirrups and twisted about to point toward a large structure made of logs. "This is your new home until the pony soldiers' big chief decides your fate. Do not try to run away or you will be shot."

In the moonlight, Birdie squinted to where he pointed. A corral filled with horses adjoined the place where she and the others were to live. A brief spasm of fear knotted her stomach. The death of her son, near starvation, the frigid cold, and the long ride to Fort Ellis had exhausted her, and she knew she had neither the strength nor the courage to run anywhere except to a warm place to rest and hopefully nourishing food.

A soldier lowered the wagon's tailgate. He waved the occupants forward. Birdie waited for her turn to jump to the ground. A pang of annoyance filled her. She bit off the oath that blistered her tongue. Neither he nor the other soldier had offered to assist the children or the frail women to the ground.

A shrill scream tore from the throat of one of the deranged women as she lifted her skirt and took flight. The soldier who had driven their wagon grabbed her by the waist. She clawed and hissed and spat like a wildcat until he slapped her and threw her to the ground. She lifted her head and screamed, "Nooooo!"

The woman's hysteria ignited a series of howls from the other demented women. Cat-shrill screams spooked the horses, causing them to whinny and rear in their traces.

The booted feet of troopers and civilians raced from buildings to fill the yard. Yodels from the terrified captives, yapping dogs, and frightened animals added to the maelstrom of voices.

Esther dashed to snatch a little girl away from the rearing hooves that would have crushed her small body.

As Birdie rushed to give aid and calm the hysterical woman, she gave an involuntary gasp as rough hands reached out to slam her against the side of the wagon. In the dark and out of sight she was pinned beneath High Eagle's brick hard body. His rough hands dug into the soft flesh of her shoulders. A shudder of revulsion ripped through her as his fetid breath and rancid body odor assailed her.

In spite of the night's chill, sweat covered her brow. The feral, wanton look in the Pawnee's eyes sent waves of nausea through her. Her head was spinning with the revelation of his evil intentions. She knew that, no matter how hard she fought, in the end he would take what he wanted.

Her voice almost cracked when she spoke. "You dung-eating son of a she-goat, I will not submit to you."

His low snigger mocked her. "Why are you so indignant, Woman with Iron Fist? You look at Thackery with yearning eyes. He will spit on you. I do not care if you were a Comanche whore. I will make you my woman." He tried to force her hand downward to touch his hardened *wasatch.*

Gasping for breath and struggling to push away from him, her piercing retort was deadly, "The first chance I get I will cut out your heart and feed it to the buzzards." She freed her hand and raked her nails across his face. "You are as filthy as your true Pawnee name—*Mud Pony!*"

He yowled against the unexpected painful attack.

While imprisoning her wrists with one hand, he wrapped the other around Birdie's throat. Just as everything was fading to a black void, from the corner of her eye she spied the fist. A jarring thud knocked the Pawnee scout to the ground. Sergeant Major Miller reached down and grabbed a handful of the scout's shirt and yanked him to his feet. He bellowed, "First Sergeant Bohanan."

A man with skin as dark as the night and wearing a soldier's uniform raced forward. "Yehsuh!"

"Place scout Levi High Eagle under arrest and escort him to the stockade. I'll write up the report."

The Negro sergeant pointed his rifle at the scout. Without shifting his stance, he asked, "What's the charge, suh?"

"There's no place in this man's outfit for molesters of women. You got that, Sergeant?"

"Yehsuh!" He prodded High Eagle in the back with the rifle barrel. "C'mon, you uppity bastard. I been itchin' for a 'scuse to shoot yo' sorry ass. I dare you to blink the wrong way."

For a terrifying flash of time, Birdie couldn't scream, breathe, or think.

****

Seeing the altercation between Sergeant Major Miller and Levi High Eagle with Birdie at the center of it, Ford Thackery jumped from the porch and double-timed across the yard. Behind him, Colonel Leland Culpepper issued orders for his junior officers to assist in bringing the melee under control.

Thackery swore under his breath as Birdie's hands reached out to grab the wagon's bed and held tight as if it were a sinking ship. Even in the darkness he could see that the blood had drained from her face, leaving it an alabaster-pale mask.

Her eyes flickered between him and Sergeant Miller and Esther, who sat on the ground, swaying back and forth as she crooned to calm the woman's madness.

As all obedient slaves do, Birdie bowed her head and awaited her fate.

Clouds billowed in the night sky, sending icy flakes. Thackery knew that soon the yard would be filled with sucking mud. He fought the urge to draw her into his arms. "Birdie?"

She hesitated before looking up at him. A small gash above her right eye bled. He fought to quell his anger. "I'm sorry you were hurt. You and the others have no need to worry. You are safe as long as you are in my care."

She shrugged, then blinked back the moisture he saw forming in her eyes. He drew a deep breath, pondering the language barrier. With High Eagle locked up, that left the Kootenai scout to translate.

Levi High Eagle's behavior disgusted Thackery. The scout's eight-year service with the Army hadn't exactly been praiseworthy. Still, the Pawnee was fluent in several native languages, which made him an asset.

This time he had overstepped moral boundaries.

"Thack-ry." Birdie's voice was almost inaudible. Yet its soft timbre caused his heart to hammer. A haunting anxiety sprang into her gaze. He wanted to earn her trust one slow step at a time. He nodded, smiling.

She pointed to him. "Thack-ry." And then to her chest. "Bur-dee. Me."

A warm glow formed in his chest. He liked the idea that she had spoken to him in the only English words she knew.

Dr. Jethro Pope limped across the yard to where Ford Thackery stood. Hot on his heels, Nora Culpepper lifted her skirts, not avoiding the muddy sludge that clung to her boots. "Captain Thackery, how can I help?"

The colonel's wife never ceased to amaze him. She was Army born and bred, and it seemed very little fazed her. She could shoot as well as any soldier, never fainted at the sight of blood, and had assisted Doc Pope in patching up more than one wounded man. And she seemed to have an innate sense of timing.

He acknowledged the woman with a nod. "Mrs. Culpepper, this is Birdie. Apparently the only English she seems to remember is her name."

He pointed to Esther. "We believe her name is either Esser or Esther. The woman she's tending is suffering from a broken mind."

He spoke briefly to the doctor. "Doc, we have five more like her."

Doctor Pope tsked as he approached Birdie. When he reached to touch the wound above her eye, she batted his hand away and made a growling sound in her throat.

The aged doctor backed away. "No telling what she and the other women have suffered. However, the wound is superficial. No stitches needed."

He glanced at Ford. "I'll see to the captives that need immediate medical attention."

Nora Culpepper sighed. "Bless be. These poor souls."

"Yes, ma'am," Thackery said. "There are other women, too. Some are Mexican, and a few Flatheads, is my guess. Regardless, when we found them they were near starved to death. We buried ten before we got to the fort. Too sick and too frail, or old. Birdie's son was among the casualties."

At the sound of her name, Birdie met them with a dubious gaze. She pointed to herself. "Bur-dee. Me." Then to Esther. "Es-ser."

"Merciful heaven. Bring these two women to my quarters." Nora Culpepper lifted her skirts to leave.

Thackery reached out and touched her arm. "I'm sorry, Mrs. Culpepper. Can't."

He was certain the back of his neck had caught fire at the strength of her searing frown. "And why not, Captain?"

He cleared his throat and shifted his stance. "First, all of the captives have to be processed and paperwork filled out. Second, every last one of them is infested with lice and no telling what other vermin; and lastly, I'm not all that certain these two won't try to run away. As best as we could surmise they were part of Chief Joseph's band. Apparently they couldn't keep up, and he left them with the promise of sending warriors to get them once the main group was safe in Canada."

Mrs. Culpepper expelled an exasperated sigh. "Why, this is outrageous rubbish. I shall speak to the colonel about this. I'm certain he will have no objections to my…"

"Now, Nora, dear," Colonel Culpepper trained an astute gaze on his wife's frowning face. "Captain Thackery is merely following protocol and obeying *my* orders."

"But Leland…"

"No buts." The tone of his voice brooked no nonsense. "These women…" He swept his hand wide. "All of these people will be treated with dignity, have warm, comfortable quarters, and plenty of nourishing food, fresh water, and coffee until they are able enough to travel."

"Not to some god-awful reservation." She placed her hands on her hips. "Aren't you even going to attempt to reconnect them with their families?"

The colonel cupped his wife's elbow. "Come along, my dear. We'll discuss this later." He cut a sharp glance toward Thackery and the doctor. "Carry on."

Thackery's voice boomed, "Sergeants Miller and Bohanan, get these people out of the weather and see to their comfort. Make sure there is fresh straw and plenty of heat in the storehouse. Pick two men to stand guard and four men to deliver hot food and beverage." Then as an afterthought, he called out, "First Sergeant Bohanan, a word."

The sergeant sprinted forward. He snapped a salute. "Cap'n?"

"You lived with the Sioux for a while, did you not?"

"I did, Cap'n. Had me a right fine wife and a

couple of young ones, too, until..." He coughed away the sudden rush of emotion.

"I'm sorry. Pasqual and his cutthroats killed a lot of good people."

"Yehsuh. Kind of you to say so, but what can I be doin' for you, Cap'n?"

"I need a translator. Someone I can trust to speak honest, and someone the women feel they can trust."

Bohanan snapped another salute. "I'll do the best I can, suh. I speak real good Sioux, Cheyenne, some Kootenai, a little Nez Perce, enough French to get by, and Pawnee. You can trust me. I don't speak with forked tongue like Levi High Eagle, and I don't altogether put much faith in Sam Two Feathers. Don't care if they did give themselves Christian names. Beggin' pardon, suh, for speakin' so bold."

Thackery turned his attention to Birdie. Esther stood, now, and still held tight to her charge. He smiled at Birdie and said, "Speak to them, Sergeant. Reassure them they won't be hurt."

Sergeant Bohanan's soft voice was like an unexpected invitation. "What is her name?" he asked in a language foreign to Thackery.

Birdie reached to touch the hand of the fearful woman. After a brief exchange, she smiled at the sergeant and then at Ford. Ford Thackery understood—Emmaline Borski.

First Sergeant Bohanan continued his oration until Birdie and Esther and the one called Emmaline followed him to the storehouse and walked inside.

Thackery willed Birdie to look at him. Instead, her spine straight and head held high, she entered the building without turning. In his entire life, he had loved one woman, and she had drowned in a sailing accident on the eve of their wedding. The painful memory made him wince, but even so he had trouble recalling Victoria's face.

He could not, he would not allow himself to fall in love with Birdie, a woman with sculpted cheekbones and eyes that he wanted to swim in. It was as if she had kissed his heart, not his lips.

Chapter Five

Lantern light cast eerie shadows along the storeroom's roughhewn walls. The large open space smelled of horse sweat, man sweat, old leather, and fresh straw. Birdie wrinkled her nose against the pungent odors as she followed the Negro sergeant through the doorway. A giant red eye flickered in a dark corner. Birdie's heart thumped. Had the white man brought them here to feed this fiend?

As her eyes adjusted to the light, she saw that the monster held fire and emitted heat. She waded through the straw to stretch her hands forward to soak up the welcomed warmth.

Sergeant Bohanan's six-foot frame cast a giant shadow. His gentle but firm voice encouraged the people to enter. At their hesitation, Birdie moved from her comfortable place to assist him. "All is well, my people. Come and find a place to rest. Soak up the warmth of the firebox."

Bohanan nodded his thanks to Birdie. He spoke long, switching back and forth from Spanish to other native languages to explain that food was on the way. He explained where to go when nature called, and that on the morrow the white medicine man would doctor them. He assured the people that the war against them was over.

A wizened man whose voice cracked with age said,

"Where will we go after this place? Will the white man herd us like sheep to another camp and then another camp until Chief Joseph cannot find us?"

"Old one, I am no predictor of tomorrow. Only the Great Spirit Father knows our fate. For your time here, fill your bellies, rest your weary souls, and dream of happy days."

A draft of cold air filled the room as four soldiers, and another with a rifle, opened the door. On a long table against a wall the men set silver trays laden with sandwiches, another with thick slices of cheese, a plate of brown disks that resembled round rocks, and two large kettles of steaming coffee, accompanied by tin mugs. Without a word, the soldiers left.

Sergeant Bohanan bid his farewells to Birdie and Esther. "Since the two of you seem to be the strongest, I put you in charge of dolin' out the food. There's plenty of wood to keep the stove goin' through the night."

He motioned for Birdie and Esther to follow him. "This is a stove." He showed them how to use the long hooked tong to lift the iron lid off the heater, and how to place pieces of wood inside the round hole. "Careful not to burn yo'selfs. Tomorrow the doctor will come to check all of you. He'll look at yer teeth, and check for ticks and such." He shuffled as if uncomfortable. "And, um, he will pr'bly need yer help wif them ladies which are touched in the head. Meanin' no disrespect." He nodded. "I'll bid you ladies g'night. If you need somethin', jes' say my name to the guard. I'll instruct him to come get me."

Birdie plucked the sleeve of his coat. "How is it you know the language of the People?"

He offered a sad smile. "Oh, when I was young,

before my hair turned the color of snow, I lived many winters with the Sioux."

"How is it that you have not forgotten the words of the Sioux when I have forgotten the language of my white mother?"

His eyes distant as if watching the past, Sergeant Bohanan spoke, "You have not forgotten, little redbird. The words are there, locked away behind a secret door in your mind. Only you hold the key to unlock this door."

"I do not understand. How can I open such a door when I don't know where to find the key?" The smile that danced in the sergeant's eyes annoyed Birdie. "Why do you laugh when I am serious? Do you mock me?"

"I do not mock you, little redbird. I laugh because the answer is here." He touched the tip of his finger to the center of her forehead. "Come, I will show you."

He motioned to Esther. "You, too."

Birdie and Esther followed him to the stove. He pointed to it and in English said, "Stove." In Nez Perce, he instructed them to repeat the word *stove* in English.

His lesson continued with the words: wood, coffee, cheese, ham, bread, woman, and soldier. His eyes shone approval as Birdie and Esther parroted each word.

He pointed to his chest. "Sergeant Isaiah Bohanan."

Their words echoed his name. "Sergeant I-zay-ah Bowl-han-an."

He chuckled. "Good 'nuff."

He held up one of the little round rocks and then popped it into his mouth and chewed, then in English said, "Cookie…good."

Again, the two women imitated his action. Both smiled as they savored the sweetness and repeated, "Cookie...good."

Sergeant Bohanan laughed loudly. "Reckon I need to be sayin' 'goodnight.'"

Immediately Birdie and Esther repeated his words.

He laughed even louder and in Nez Perce said, "We'll keep workin'."

Before he opened the door and stepped into the night, Esther called his name. He met her with a questioning gaze.

She hesitated, her hands clasped together. Then in a quiet, timid voice, she tested her memory. "Thank you."

Birdie, too, said, "Saaa...thank you."

"Saaa, in English is 'yes', Miz Birdie."

She offered him a teary smile. "Yes, thank you."

****

Birdie loosed an explosive sigh. "No, you do not need to hoard the sandwiches. Eat. There will be more food tomorrow."

An old woman offered Birdie a withering sneer. "You may have lived among the People since you were a weanling, but you are not of us. You might believe the forked-tongue promises of the white-eyes. I do not."

Esther exchanged disgusted glances with Birdie. "You speak foolish words, old one. Eventually the food you have squirreled away will turn rancid and will cramp your stomach when you eat it. Later you will not be able to enjoy the fresh food the pony soldiers bring because you will be squatting behind a tree emptying your bowels and crying for the gods to ease your pain."

Esther picked up a brown disk. "This is a cookie.

In my other life I made dozens of them for my wretched husband and his two terrible sons." She grabbed a handful and distributed them among the children. "Eat. Cookies will make you happy."

Birdie was hungry enough to savor each morsel of the salty ham sandwiches and wedges of cheese. The coffee scalded her parched throat as she swallowed it; still she felt frozen inside. The mug's heat warmed her chilled fingers. She lifted the tin cup to her lips and blew gently until the hot surface rippled with little waves. She half closed her eyes, savoring the hot fragrant steam that wafted up to her face. To finish the most luscious meal of her life she savored the one remaining cookie. To herself and in English she said, "Cookie."

Before claiming a place to rest, she stood before the stove and fed it slivers of wood until she had gradually increased the size of the fire. The warmth soothed her weary limbs and gave her renewed hope. Gradually, life returned to her muscles; the warmth from the stove was the most wonderful fire in the whole world. She stretched her arms, stood, and dangled the damp hem of her dress forward to dry.

Settling in the straw, she pondered the words of the Negro sergeant about how it was up to her to find the key to her forgotten language. Eyelids heavy, weighted with sleep, they closed at last, and Birdie slept.

She twitched. *This isn't real.* Dreams loosed in sleep are like curtains pulled aside. *See a mist clearing. Covered wagons form a circle. A woman wearing an apron hovers over a campfire. She hums. A boy of about two years and with orange hair sits on the ground playing with a toy. The woman says, "I'm baking you an upside-down berry corncake for your birthday. My goodness, Birdie Mae, I can hardly believe you are five years old. Time does fly."*

The girl with red pigtails is holding a sock doll and singing, "Ring around the rosies, a pocketful of posies..."

Now the man is yelling and there is more yelling. The woman is screaming, "Hide, Birdie! Grab Tommy and hide!" The man grabs his rifle. He doesn't shoot. A bright red spot spreads across his blue shirt. The woman runs toward him and calls, "Thomas!"

A half-naked man with a frightful face striped with red and yellow paint runs over the woman with his horse, a brown-and-white pinto. The Indian reaches down and lifts Tommy into his arms.

The girl is searching, searching. The key...where is the key?

An eagle flies overhead. Something silver gleams in its talons. The key.

The girl turns and Birdie sees a face.

The girl's eyes are red-rimmed and bespoke her sadness as if she too, in her own child's way, had come to understand that the memory would never again return to life and there was no further reason to stay in this place.

Birdie gasps when she realizes she is looking at herself.

The girl stretches on tiptoes to grasp the key, and then freezes with terror as a warrior with a wicked face rides forward and scoops her into his arms.

She fought the hand shaking her shoulder. "Birdie...Birdie. Awake. You are moaning. It is a bad dream."

Her eyes opened. She gulped for air and managed to calm herself enough to think. When the fog in her brain cleared and she realized where she was, she said, "Es-ser," and then whimpered, "I saw it. All of it."

Esther wrapped her arms around the shivering girl. "Tell me of this dream." She pushed to her knees. "I will get us coffee. You feed the fire."

As they settled with hands wrapped around mugs of strong, tepid coffee, Birdie related the dream. "I had a baby brother. His name was Toe-me. The man was my father. Mother called him—Thomas. My name is Birdie Mae. I must try to remember my mother's name."

And then as if the weight of remembering that horrible time when she was kidnapped was too much to bear, she wept.

Chapter Six

Morning came, cold and somber. The acrid smell of wood smoke hovered over the compound. Slowly, Fort Ellis awoke with the bugler's first call of reveille.

The people inside the storeroom rubbed sleep from their eyes. Birdie pulled the blanket tighter around her body. The fire in the stove had gone cold. Outside, a brisk wind howled around the buildings and reminded her of baying wolves. Reluctantly, she rose from her straw nest and hurried to remove the heavy iron lid from the stove and poke the ashes until she awakened a live ember. Blowing gently, she fed slender slivers of kindling until timid flames flicked hungry tongues as if begging for more wood.

She meandered to the window and peered out, her eyes adjusting to the darkness. Lines of soldiers jumped up and down in a macabre dance while a lone soldier yelled at them. More soldiers marched back and forth in the slushy snow. She wondered if they were cold, and why didn't they stay inside around a stove.

All was so foreign to her. She had much to learn.

Her thoughts flashed back to the little round sweetness she had savored last night. A smile tugged at her lips and in English she shouted, "Cook-ie."

Esther pulled the blanket from over her head to peer squint-eyed at Birdie. "You shriek like screech owl."

"Ah-ho," Birdie laughed with glee. "I am remembering. This is good, no?"

"Saaa...most good." Esther crawled from her blanket. "I need to go to the place to relieve myself. Come with me."

"Saaa...means yes," Birdie reminded Esther.

****

Captain Ford Thackery and Dr. Jethro Pope sat across the desk from Colonel Leland Culpepper as they discussed what to do with the volunteer captives.

Pope tapped his fingers together. "My first priority, of course, is to examine the six women whose minds are broken." He looked at Thackery. "Ford, if they cannot communicate, as you say, what about the other two women? Can they explain to us what happened to cause this type of terrible malaise?"

Ford toyed with the handle of his coffee mug. "Although Birdie and Esther are white, I'm afraid they've been captive so long that neither of them remembers English."

"You've relegated Scout High Eagle to the guard house. Because of the charges against him, he will remain there until we decide his fate. What about Scout Two Feathers to communicate with them?"

"Good idea, Jethro," Colonel Culpepper quipped.

Ford neither smiled nor frowned. "I'm not sure I trust the Kootenai scout, Leland. Plus, the women seem afraid of him."

"Then who?" Jethro's reply was tersely spoken.

Ford's gaze was stern when he answered the doctor. "Sergeant Isaiah Bohanan speaks a variety of native languages. Besides, from all observations, the women are comfortable in his presence. He's one of my best men, and I trust him."

"You have a point, Ford." Leland continued, "I'll have Mrs. Culpepper gather clothing from some of the other wives for these women. I will leave it to her to arrange for bathing tubs, hot water, and soap, as well recruiting some of the…ah…less squeamish ladies to assist with fripperies such as head washing and de-licing." He cut his attention toward the doctor. "That is if you have no objection, Jethro."

The doctor held his hands forward. "Cleanliness is next to godliness. All the help I can get will make my examinations easier."

Ford chuckled. "Begging your pardons, the demented women don't like being touched, especially by strangers. I'm afraid if Mrs. Culpepper and her ladies go trooping in with well-intentioned designs, you will have a cat-squalling, cat-spitting fight on your hands." He laughed again. "Believe me, I've witnessed it. Poor Trooper Dennis thought a cougar had hold of him when the woman called Emmaline attacked him."

Leland Culpepper sputtered. "Well…what do you suggest? We can't risk a lice infestation or some other disease at the fort. My only other alternative is to keep them locked up, and I can't keep them here forever, and I certainly can't turn them out."

Jethro Pope slowly nodded. "There is a new sanitarium for the mentally unbalanced, located in Warm Springs." He did a quick mental calculation. "It's approximately one hundred seven miles from the fort." He shifted toward the colonel. "Leland, are you willing to spare two trustworthy troopers, the ambulance wagon with two horses, plus supplies? If so, I believe inside of a week we can find professional medical assistance for these poor souls until their families can be located."

Colonel Culpepper slapped his hands on his desk. "Let's make it so, Jethro. Send a telegram, at once, to the heads of this institution explaining our need and ask for an immediate reply."

Ford cleared his throat. "We still have the problem of baths, sir." An unexpected desire thickened his veins and he immediately crossed his legs and squeezed his inner thighs tight at the thought of Birdie wearing nothing but a smile. He shifted straighter in the chair to ease the discomfort from the throbbing bulge between his legs. He cleared the rasp from his throat. "The two women, Birdie and Esther, have a way with all the captives. May I suggest we get them cleaned up first and then have Sergeant Bohanan assist in explaining how they can help us?"

"Excellent...excellent, Ford." Leland Culpepper rubbed his hands together. "If it weren't so early in the morning, I'd pour a round of bourbon to celebrate the solution to a rather delicate conundrum."

Dr. Jethro Pope chortled. "As the fort physician, I prescribe bourbon-laced coffee to, ah, ward off an oncoming chill."

****

After suffering through three days of monotonous routine, Birdie again stared into the breaking of dawn. Patches of snow glistened in the morning rays. A new day, she thought. A tear slid down her cheek as she still ached with the death of her son. One half of her heart was happy that Ashkii now walked with the soul keepers; the other half wrestled with shame because she was glad that he had died.

After the nightmare of her family's slaughter and

when sleep finally came, the face of Thackery had visited her in another dream. She had shed tears for the girl forever in the past and for the woman who had suddenly realized she had a woman's needs. A woman's desires.

Then she spotted Thackery standing on the porch talking to a man, holding a black bag, who clapped Thackery on the back. She was not a woman of flowery rhymes. No such words existed in the People's language, but the sight of him covered her with pleasure, like warm water. He looked especially fine as he flashed a smile and spoke to a group of passing women, eliciting laughter as they acknowledged him.

He looked toward the storehouse, and though he could not see her staring at him, his gaze seemed to settle on her. She could not look away, just as she had not been able to stop thinking about him since that day in the Gallatins when he had looked deep into her eyes and had gently traced the scar on her cheek.

Her cheeks burned as he and the other man stepped off the porch. Sergeant Bohanan joined the men and conversed for a moment before they approached the building.

"Esther, come quick."

Esther peered over Birdie's shoulder and let out an anguished sigh. "They do not smile. Maybe this is bad."

"No food has been brought this morning. Do you think we are to be lined up and shot? At least that is what the old ones have been whispering these nights past."

"Bah, what do they know?"

"Whatever Thackery is about, it can't be any worse than perishing from boredom."

47

Birdie's comment elicited a snicker from Esther. "Come." She locked hands with Birdie. "Whatever it is, we will face it together."

Birdie reached up and traced the deep scar that marred her face and neck. "Yes, life is full of hurts. Like it or not, we have to learn to live with them."

Birdie's pulse pounded faster when the door opened. Thackery had to stoop to keep from hitting his head when he entered.

"Good morning, Birdie...Esther." Butterflies winged their way to Birdie's stomach at his low, sensuous tone.

She nodded. "Thack-ry," she whispered, trying to catch her breath, lost in the wake of her appreciative appraisal as her gaze raked over the broad shoulders that filled out his uniform jacket, over the pants that hugged his muscled legs, and the gun belt strapped around his lean hips.

He shifted his glance to the people who stood with anticipation in their eyes as if facing a firing squad. He cleared his throat and spoke a long time to Sergeant Bohanan, gesturing often.

Birdie understood her name. Her heart broke into a hard gallop.

Bohanan stepped forward. He motioned with his hands for the people to sit. He reassured them with a smile. He pointed and spoke in Nez Perce, "This is Captain Thackery. You already know him. You know me." He pointed to himself, and then to the doctor. "This is Fort Ellis's medicine man. He is called Dr. Pope. He is not here to hurt you, only to ask your name, your age, and to look at your teeth, inside your ears, and to listen to your heart with a snake called a-a..." he looked at the doctor for help.

"Stethoscope." Dr. Pope opened his bag and removed the stethoscope and held it up for all to see.

Bohanan spoke to the doctor. "Keep the bag open, suh, and if'n you have little pill bottles, hold 'em up."

Pope nodded his understanding.

"This is the medicine man's magic bag. In it he has many potions. All are good." Bohanan directed his attention to Birdie and Esther. "Cap'n Thackery respectfully requests that you ladies help the doctor as much as you can."

Birdie arched an auburn brow. "But how, when we know so few Eng-lish words?"

"Now, don't you worry 'bout that, little redbird. I'se be here to hep you."

She glanced at Esther. A spasm of hesitation crossed Esther's face until she nodded.

Isaiah said, "We can begin when you are ready, Doctor."

A warm gleam sparkled in Ford Thackery's eyes. "I have other duties. Please excuse me." He spoke to the doctor and the sergeant, and left.

Dr. Pope said he wanted to process the white captives first. "We need to get their information and get them cleaned up as soon as possible. I expect to hear from the sanitarium in Warm Springs any day."

Bohanan nodded his understanding and then translated to Birdie and Esther.

The four of them gingerly picked their way through the crowd to a darkened corner in the rear of the storehouse. Six bedraggled skeletons huddled together and stared with vacant eyes.

"My god," sputtered the doctor.

Birdie squatted. She gently lifted a bony hand to her cheek and spoke in a quiet monotone. When she finished, she said, "Her name is Patricia Sherman. She is thirty-six years old. She was a schoolteacher. The Comanche attacked the school. They left no girls alive and took only the strongest boys and her. She thinks it was five years ago."

As if the memories were too great, Patricia Sherman placed the blanket over her head and, moaning, rocked back and forth.

"I need to examine her." Pope squatted and opened his bag.

Bohanan said, "Meaning no disrespect, suh, but if'n you don't want to set her to squallin', I'd leave the 'zamination till 'nother time. Why don't we jest let Miz Birdie get their info'mation first."

"Of course, that's sounds reasonable."

The sergeant nodded to Birdie while Esther hurried to get a bowl of water and a rag to soothe the mentally wounded woman.

Birdie moved to a blanketed lump. She motioned for the doctor to stand back, and for the sergeant to join her. He translated while she spoke. "She had…" Birdie struggled to find the word, "…little brown spots on her face."

"Freckles?"

"Yes, freckles. They tried to burn them off her face."

"Who are 'they'—the Nez Perce?"

"No. We found her. She was left to die. It would have been better if the Great Father Spirit had claimed her."

"What is her name?"

50

Birdie shrugged. "We do not know. She cannot speak."

"Ask if she can write her name."

In a second, Birdie nodded.

Bohanan asked the doctor for pencil and paper. He handed it to the woman. Four pairs of eyes watched as a gnarled hand clutched the pencil. It seemed to take much effort until she scrawled across the paper and held it forward.

Dr. Pope asked, "What does it say?"

Bohanan read, "Ugly Woman, once wife of Seth Cartwright."

Dr. Pope carefully peeled the blanket away from her face. What he saw roiled his stomach. Her face had been brutally seared, leaving the skin puckered like old leather, marring her beauty forever.

"I won't hurt you." He schooled himself against the lipless face mottled with thickened scars. "Mrs. Cartwright, what is your Christian name?"

She wrote, "Nancy."

"I am sorry for your suffering, Nancy Cartwright. We will try to find your husband."

She loosed the keening in her throat; the pleading in her eyes spoke volumes. And then she pulled the blanket over her head.

"I understand." Dr. Pope's voice was filled with compassion.

The group moved to the next woman. Clara Butler opened her mouth to reveal sickly pink, toothless gums. She hawked and spat on Sergeant Bohanan.

The slow process of identification lasted several hours, gaining the names of: Minnie Sudbury, who unexpectedly launched herself toward the doctor's leg and latched on with the strength of a snapping turtle; Lucy Nelson, who dissolved into a fit of giggles; and Emmaline, who screamed, "Emmaline Borski. My baby…my baby." She repeated the phrase over and over and over.

Following the routine, Bohanan squatted. She launched a full-body attack, bowling him over. He grabbed both her wrists to keep her from clawing out his eyes.

Her high-pitched screams and snarls created a panic. The old people set up their own yodels and screaming, "*Brujo.*"

Two armed guards slammed back the storehouse doors, rifles jacked tight against their shoulders. Dr. Pope, yelled, "No! Don't shoot. Put down your weapons and get that madwoman off the sergeant."

It took the efforts of Birdie and Esther to calm the people.

Ford Thackery raced through the open door. He reached down to assist the sergeant to his feet. "What the hell is happening?"

Sergeant Bohanan's face was a bloody mess of long fingernail gouges. "Lawd a'mighty, Cap'n. I b'lieve I done messed my drawers. Reckon I need a coupla stiff whiskeys to steady my nerves."

Sergeant Miller burst through the opening. "Esther!"

She pushed through the huddle and grabbed his outstretched hand. "Miller, I-I…"

"Sergeant Miller! Leave your personal feelings at the door."

"Yessir!" He patted Esther's cheek. "I understand, Cap'n."

Thackery's face creased into a troubled frown. A tense moment passed between them when Birdie stepped forward to face him. In an instant her green eyes collided with the deep blue of his. The emerald eyes that had seemed so bright with anticipation darkened with disappointment as if she knew there was no way he could come to her.

"Captain Thackery, in all my years of practice I have amputated arms and legs and been elbow deep in blood. The mistreatment of these women is—inhuman."

"You don't know the half of it, Doctor, nor do I, for that matter." Thackery glanced at Birdie and Esther. "You could ask them, but why make them relive their own hell?"

"Yes, of course. I'm a medical doctor, a surgeon, not a psychiatrist. However, sometimes talking about one's deepest mental hurts helps to heal the mind."

"Not today, Jethro, not today."

"The sooner the better, Ford. We both know it."

When Thackery didn't answer, the doctor said, "I will put valerian drops in their coffee to calm them. At least we'll be able to get them bathed and into clean garments without more hysterical outbursts."

"When?"

"During breakfast." Dr. Pope directed his attention to Miller and Bohanan. "Have six number two washtubs brought to the infirmary. Go by the galley and order as many kettles of hot water as the cook can spare. Instruct him to heat more."

Thackery's lips lifted in a sardonic smile. "Too bad you didn't think of the valerian earlier, Doc."

"Yes, Captain, you've made your point."

"Better get those drops ready. The food is about to

arrive." Thackery left the storehouse to seek his own breakfast.

"Sergeant Bohanan, follow me to the infirmary. I'll tend to your face. Some of those scratches look pretty deep."

The sergeant heaved a sigh. "Yehsuh." He looked about in the semi-dark interior. "I got me a feelin' sumpin' ain't jest right."

Dr. Pope harrumphed. "Something isn't just right, I agree, about this whole situation. Come to the infirmary as soon as you can. We don't want those wounds to fester." He drew his collar around his neck and stepped into the morning's cold.

Isaiah was taken by complete surprise when Birdie boldly grabbed his arm. "I'se got to go, little redbird." He patted her hand. "Food'll be here in a minute. I'll come get ya'll later."

"There is another one."

"Another what?"

"She is like you."

"What do yo mean, she's like me?"

Birdie pointed. "There. She is like you. Hair like the buffalo."

Isaiah followed Birdie, gingerly picking his way so as not to step on anyone until Birdie squatted and spoke at length to a figure huddled under a blanket. She looked up at Isaiah, concern shining in her eyes.

Birdie said, "She is afraid she will be punished more."

Isaiah Bohanan lowered his tall frame to the floor. He murmured gently. "You speak English?"

Two tawny eyes in a walnut-brown face stared at him and then with hesitation at Birdie, who said, "She came from the Cheyenne. They traded her for two appaloosa horses. She is a little bit young and a little bit old, like Esther."

Isaiah spoke again, this time in Cheyenne. "My name is Isaiah. What are you called?"

She lowered the blanket. "I was once called Ja'meena Pickett. Now I am Black Frog."

He offered a kind smile. "No one here will harm you. You have my word." His voice gentle, he turned and continued, "Miz Birdie, Miz Esther, I 'preciate it if'n you take good care of Miz Ja'meena Picket. It's been a long time since my ole eyes has seen a woman of my kind."

Chapter Seven

Two hours later, with Sergeant Bohanan in the lead, Birdie and the six deranged women, all holding hands, and with Esther and Ja'meena bringing up the rear, brought curious spectators as the women walked single file across the snowy yard to the infirmary.

Before entering, Bohanan fidgeted with his cap. "Doc, I don't feel comfort'ble bein' here with these ladies even if'n they are gonna be behind a bunch of blankets. 'Tain't decent."

Dr. Pope cocked an eyebrow as he finished wrapping a strand of wire around a nail. "It seems I'm no longer in charge."

"Pshaw to both of you. Now, stop being such a fuddy-duddy, Isaiah Bohanan," Nora Culpepper scolded, "and help me hang these quilts. They will act as curtains. You will be seated behind it and facing the door. You won't see the ladies and they will not see you. Besides, I'm not so altogether certain that if you were looking they'd know the difference. Poor souls, their minds all locked up in some kind of twisted torment." She harrumphed. "You just be ready to hand Dr. Pope buckets of water when we call for them, and to translate when needed."

"Yesum, jes' the same—"

"Hush up, Isaiah, and that's an order." The crispness in Nora Culpepper's voice was enough to chill the already cold air.

With the help of Bohanan's translation, Nora Culpepper explained that Birdie and Esther were to help her with undressing and bathing all the women and washing their hair. "Then afterwards, when they're settled, the two of you will have fresh water for your own baths."

"Where will we wash the clothes?" Birdie's voice was a soft inquisitive whisper.

Nora wrinkled her nose. "We have new dresses for all of you. Hand-me-downs, but lovingly used." Quietly aside, she said, "Isaiah, tell Birdie to toss the rags in a pile, and afterwards, please discreetly burn them. They are virtually crawling with vermin."

"Yes'um."

Some of the women laughed out right, and some expelled pleasurable sighs as they sat in the tubs of hot water. Not one resisted as Birdie, Esther, and Ja'meena set about scrubbing filth-crusted bodies.

"Nora, oh, Nora, dear, I've come with the dresses and to lend a hand." Nora Culpepper cringed at the annoying shrill of Elmira Ledbetter's voice. She cast a doleful glance toward the ceiling as the stout woman waltzed in like she owned the infirmary. Elmira prattled on, "Mrs. Bradbury is a bit squeamish about being around crazy people. I said to her, 'On my great-granny's garters, Wilma, insanity isn't contagious.' "

Nora Culpepper gave the makeshift curtain a vicious yank to draw it shut. She fisted her hands against her hips. "Shut your mouth, Elmira. We both know your curiosity is about to eat you alive. The only reason you're here is to gawk at these poor women and then run out and spread your vicious gossip." She pointed to a nearby chair. "Leave the dresses there."

Displeasure narrowed Elmira's eyes. She responded flippantly, "You may be a colonel's wife, but you hold no rank over me or any of the other ladies at the fort."

"Ah, Miz Ledbetter?"

Impatience tinged Elmira's voice. "What is it, Sergeant?"

"If'n you don't mind my sayin', deez women been through hell 'n' back. Mebbe give 'em time to—"

Elmira's lips curled into a sarcastic smile. "I do mind your saying, Sergeant Bohanan. Your knowledge of women wouldn't fill a thimble."

Elmira grabbed two dresses. She pivoted away and waddled across the room, her broad hips swaying with the motion as she neared one of the tubs.

Birdie and Esther clutched hands and backed away.

Isaiah warned, "Miz Ledbetter, if'n I were you—"

Elmira cut him off with a glare as she approached a woman of mere skin and bone who sat in water that barely covered her meager breasts. Her mousy brown hair hung lank and straggly.

Isaiah seated himself behind the curtain of quilts. He muttered, "Don't say I didn't try to warn you."

A smile curved Elmira's lips. She spoke slowly, enunciating each word. "Hello. I am Mrs. Elmira Ledbetter. I have brought clean clothing. You may have first pick of the dresses."

Emmaline twisted her thin fingers in provoked disquiet as she glanced around the room from woman to woman.

Elmira Ledbetter reached out and grabbed one of Emmaline's hands. Her voice syrupy sweet, she said, "I truly find it hard to believe that you stayed with the savages instead of trying to escape. Why I—"

Emmaline's eyes glittered dangerously in the dappled light. She fixed a cold glower on Elmira Ledbetter.

Birdie braced herself for what was about to follow, for she sensed it wouldn't be pleasant.

With an angry snort, Emmaline launched herself from the tub, knocking Elmira Ledbetter to the floor and sending a geyser of water to splash over them. Dripping wet and naked, Emmaline straddled Elmira's dumpy body.

Elmira screamed, "She's killing me! Get this disgusting, crazy savage off me!"

Nora yelled for the doctor. Isaiah knocked over his chair as he flung himself out of it. He got tangled in the curtain and in fighting his way clear pulled the wire off the nail. The heavy quilts dropped to the floor, exposing all of the women.

"Yes...I'm crazy...crazy," Emmaline's maniacal laughter grew louder, "bedbug crazy."

Springing to action, Birdie and Esther grabbed Emmaline by the waist in time to keep her from sinking bared teeth into Elmira Ledbetter's neck. The effort sent Birdie and Esther stumbling backward over the area of soapy water. Abruptly slipping and sliding, their feet skidded and propelled them across the room. Esther landed hard on her derriere. Birdie winced as her head hit the wooden wall.

Isaiah felt like he was skating on ice when his boots nearly slipped out from under him as he rushed to grab Emmaline around the waist and hauled her off the sobbing Elmira. "I tried to warn yo', Miz Ledbetter."

Emmaline leaned down and clamped her teeth into Isaiah's hand. He yowled in pain and dropped her to the floor.

Weeping bitterly, Elmira bustled from the infirmary, her shoes squishing and sliding, her blue skirts flapping wetly around her legs. She pushed past Ford Thackery, nearly bowling him over.

"You should be court-martialed for bringing those…those deranged creatures here." Her wail grew louder.

Thackery caught the edge of the door and swept it forward. It banged against the jamb. "What the devil is going on here?" he bellowed.

Ja'meena raced headlong to grab one of the quilts. She held it forward and spoke rapidly to the naked women. Emmaline snatched the patchwork coverlet from Ja'meena's outstretched hands, pulled it around her shivering body, and then stepped inside the tub and sat down.

The infirmary increased into a bevy of hysteria with Birdie, Esther, and Ja'meena darting from tub to tub trying to quell the disturbance.

Dr. Pope issued a set of instructions to Isaiah, who rattled off in Pawnee, "Birdie, try to get Emmaline to drink this. It will calm her. The doc has more for the others. Understand?"

Birdie's eyes widened, she took the cup and said, "Ah-ho."

Ja'meena offered Isaiah a cautious look. The words she spoke came slow but clear. "I speak English. I help, too?"

Isaiah cupped her face. "Girl, you are an angel." He nodded his consent.

"What in the name of Hades is all this caterwauling?" Colonel Culpepper immediately did an about-face at the sight of wet, scar-pocked, naked bodies. His voice, colored with a flare of anger, commanded, "Nora, for God's sake, get these women covered."

She hastily fired off, "Don't yell at me. This is all Elmira's doing."

Sergeant Bohanan waved Sergeant Miller outside. "We ain't needed in there. 'Tain't decent nohow, seein' them ladies in their jaybird suits."

Nora Culpepper shooed her husband and Ford Thackery out. "Your presence is not needed."

It was as if Ford beseeched Birdie to look at him. She deliberately refused, waiting until he walked to the door. She looked at his back, drawn irresistibly to his virile power and manly grace.

She mimicked Nora's actions by saying, "Shoo…shoo."

Esther and Ja'meena filled tin mugs while Dr. Pope laced the coffee with valerian.

Later, the six unstable but subdued women were encouraged to each select a dress from the pile of hand-me-downs. Birdie and the others assisted Nora in brushing and braiding hair that had been scrubbed clean with lye soap and the lice nits removed.

While picking through the pile of gowns, Emmaline Borski fell to her knees and crawled on her belly to reach underneath a tall medicine cabinet.

"No, Emmaline, you'll get dirty. There's no more clean water." Birdie knelt beside the woman.

"Careful, Birdie, she might explode any minute," Esther warned.

Emmaline pulled a dust-covered doll from beneath the cabinet and clutched it to her breast. Her sobs rose to a mournful wail. Tears slid down her cheeks as she rocked back and forth. "My baby. My baby." Her whispers were furtive as she kissed the doll's dirty face. "Don't you worry, Suzie. Mama won't let them take you away."

"Merciful heavens." Nora sobbed. "She thinks it's a real baby."

Dr. Pope rushed from his office. He spotted the doll. "That's Judy Mason's dolly. We searched high and low and couldn't find it, and all the time it was under the medicine cabinet." He reached out.

Emmaline stiffened; her expression darkened.

"Leave her be, Jethro." Nora blurted out. "If a tattered sock doll gives Mrs. Borski peace, then who are you to deny her that bit of comfort?"

Emmaline allowed Birdie to lead her to a cot. She lay down, and her expression immediately changed, becoming open and innocent as she cuddled the little sock doll that had a missing button eye.

Chapter Eight

The tub was small, and Birdie was forced to dangle her legs over the outside edge. She felt dirty, bedraggled, and completely out of sorts. The tub was filled to nearly overflowing with steamy water as Nora Culpepper poured the last drops from the enormous blue speckled kettle. Birdie stared at Nora in astonishment as the colonel's wife disappeared into another room. It was incomprehensible that this woman of importance should serve her and Esther and Ja'meena as if she were their slave.

Settling in the tub, she closed her eyes, and positively reveled in the hot water. As she leaned her head back against the tub's edge, her mind filled with a fleeting memory of a red-haired woman on her knees next to a tub of hot water with Birdie in it. The woman said, *"Birdie, this is important. I want you to remember."* Birdie nodded, though she had closed her eyes to keep soap from getting into them while her mother washed her hair. *"Your last name is Dix. Spell it with me: D-i-x. Dix. Can you remember?"*

"Yes, Mommy, D-i-x. Dix."

"Oh, my dear, why ever are you crying? Aren't you enjoying your bath?" Nora Culpepper asked with a concerned smile.

She opened her eyes in startled surprise and stared up at the woman. "My name...Birdie Mae Dix. D-i-x."

"Marvelous." Nora spun about and bustled to the doctor's office. She rapped on the door and without waiting for an answer, opened the door. "Jethro, her name is Birdie Mae Dix. I must tell the colonel."

An hour later, Birdie, Esther, and Ja'meena lifted sandwiches from a tray and went to find a corner in the infirmary to sit. "No...no." Nora frowned. "Civilized ladies do not sit on the floor."

She pulled four chairs from the table and motioned with her hand. Containing her frustration, she said, "Surely, one of you remembers table manners from your past."

Esther and Ja'meena exchanged glances and nodded. Esther spoke to Birdie. The three of them walked to the table and sat. Nora sighed in relief as she joined them. As they dined on roast beef sandwiches, cups of strong black coffee, and a dozen butter cookies, Nora named each food and they repeated the words after her.

Nora continued, "Ja'meena is a lovely name. How long were you captive?"

Ja'meena smiled at the colonel's wife. "My mother used to say that curiosity killed the cat." Ja'meena paused, hesitated. "Forgive me for being impertinent. It's been four years since I was taken. I seem to have lost my manners."

Nora toyed with a spoon. "It is I who should apologize. But if you don't mind my asking, how much English do Esther and Birdie understand?"

At the sound of her name, Birdie's face angled upward. "Me...Birdie Mae Dix."

Ja'meena exchanged words with Esther. She murmured, "Esther was captive for more than twenty winters, which means twenty years. She was twenty-five when the Hunkpapa stole her. She tried to hold on to her English, but like the sun in winter it faded away. Now she tries to remember."

"And Birdie?" Nora asked.

This time the exchange of words seemed to go on forever. Finally, Ja'meena said, "Birdie remembers a cake her mother baked for her birthday. She was five when the Pawnee came. That was eighteen winters ago. The only word she remembers is her name, and the names of her family—Tommy, Thomas, and Mommy."

Nora tsked. "The poor child."

Birdie concentrated on the words exchanged between her friends and the colonel's wife. She seemed to withdraw almost visibly into herself. Their words were like a meandering river with all manner of interesting twists and turns, none of which she understood.

Birdie yawned. She blinked. It was still day and not time for sleeping. She yawned again. Her eyelids drooped against her will. She did not see the sly exchange of smiles between Nora Culpepper and Dr. Pope who stood nearby with a small glass bottle in his hand.

She didn't remember being led to a cot, or lying down, or having a quilt tucked around her.

A dream passed in a blurred rush. She heard the pleasant hypnotic hum of cicadas on a drowsy summer evening and imagined Ford's fingers touching her in the cool of the night. She sensed her need—the hunger curling along her loins in a slow provocative rush. Her physical need of Ford was like hunger, a primitive cry to fill the emptiness within. Yet underlying it was the stirring of some far deeper emotion.

She chastised herself. Ford Thackery had been generous and kind, and nothing else. She saw herself angry and impatient when she suddenly imagined herself as his woman. And then the muted screams of tortured souls drifted down to haunt her, and try as she might, she could not block them out.

****

Several hours later, Ford sat with the others in the Culpepper's parlor while Nora served coffee. Leland Culpepper said, "It's been more than an eventful day. Nora, my dear, thank you for going the extra mile. You are a real trooper. I know you are exhausted. Why don't you retire for the rest of the evening?"

"Good heavens!" Her face alive with mischief, his wife replied, "These ladies are in my charge. Whatever you have to say, I'm entitled to hear." She settled in her favorite rocking chair.

"So be it, then. Since Sergeant Bohanan has intimate knowledge of life among the Indians, we have asked him to give us an accounting of possible tragedies that all of the captives have suffered, especially those we will transport to the sanitarium in Warm Springs. You may find some of what he relates rather gruesome and upsetting."

"As you well know, I am not a shrinking violet, Leland," she demurred in a mock scold. "Sergeant Bohanan, don't you dare hold back. No matter how horrible, tell it like it is."

The Negro sergeant cut his eyes toward his captain. Thackery gave him a slight nod of assurance.

"What is it ya'll wants to know? This might hep me to get started."

Dr. Pope said, "Why are children and women taken captive? With their bodies crisscrossed with scars, I can only imagine the hardships these women endured, but what is it that drives some of them mad, like Emmaline Borski and Patricia Sherman, and how do others like Birdie and Esther and Ja'meena manage to hold on to their sanity?"

Nora's voice was meek but earnest. "Ja'meena has given me a little insight into their lives. Still, I wonder why is it that they, all of them, didn't try to escape?"

Isaiah removed his cap and set it on the table beside his cup and saucer. He stood and walked to look out at the yard, massaging his temples as if feeling a headache coming on. "The Comanche, they will ride a thousand miles jes' to wipe out a settlement. The Pawnee, they're known for their cruelty, and they likes to brand their women. The X that trails down Miz Birdie's face is Sacred Killer's brand. Even though he claimed her as his woman, it don't mean she was treated kindly. No, suh. 'Though she was spared a lot of terrible indignities, that other scar, the one that trails down the side of her neck, was mos' likely made when Sacred Killer ousted an older and jealous wife from his lodge. Miz Birdie pro'bly had to fight for her life. Mos' likely had to fight every day to stay alive. The native women, well, they sometimes meaner'n the warriors."

He stopped to organize his thoughts. "I'm not used to givin' long speeches."

"You're doing fine, Sergeant. Continue," Ford prompted.

"Yehsuh. The tribes don't jes' make war on settlers, they war with each other. When settlements are raided and chil'ren stolen, it's to replace the Ind'an children that have either died from disease or been killed. Onct the young'uns are taken, the ones that can't keep up, or whines and cries all the time, well…" He looked down at his boots. "They don't survive, if you take my meanin'.

"Same goes for captive women. Sometimes so many Ind'an women die in childbirth, disease, or in war that there ain't enough to satisfy the carnal needs of the warriors, or to take to wife to bear chil'ren. So the warriors go on raids and kidnap women—old, young, ugly, pretty—it don't matter.

"They're made slaves. They're beaten daily, like dogs, and worked like mules, and…" He drew a shuddering breath. "I don't 'xactly know how the dividin' up goes, but certain captive women are chosen to be concubines." Beads of sweat lined his forehead. "Beggin' pardon, Miz Culpepper, ma'am."

Her voice was a quiet whisper. "It's all right, Isaiah. Please continue."

"Yessum. When the warriors come back from raiding, their blood is hot with lust. All the concubines are taken to the fornicatin' lodge and they are…." He scrubbed large mahogany hands over his face. "They are ridden the way stallions ride mares—sometimes for several days without stopping—and when the frenzy is over, these poor women are still 'spected to cook and chop wood, even when they are heavy with child.

"As for why they don't try to escape—miles from nowhere and sometimes traded from tribe to tribe and traipsed from territory to territory, how would the women know where to go? And when they got there, how would they live, with no money an' no one to care for 'em? And stealing a horse is a killin' offense, but she wouldn't get far on foot. They stay 'cause, bad as it is, they got no choice…'cept for takin' their own life. And more'n you know do that."

He drew the blue floral demitasse cup to his lips and drained the contents in one long swallow. "Cap'n, suh, I can't tell no mo'. Court martial me if you must, but don't make me tell anymo'."

Leland Culpepper poured a whiskey and handed it to the sergeant. No one spoke. It was as if the silence was trying to absorb the aftershocks of the sergeant's account.

The parlor door swung open and banged against the wall. A shrill voice announced, "Nora, I heard there was a meeting going on, and I thought I'd pop in to see if you were planning the social for Saturday night." Indignity dripped from the woman's voice. "Telling me must have slipped your mind."

"Get out, Elmira. Get out! And don't *ever* enter my home again without first knocking." Nora Culpepper flew at the woman, grabbing her by the shoulders and shoving her from the room. She slammed the door, and then turned to meet the men's aggravated expressions. She huffed, "Forgive me, but Elmira Ledbetter is a *pain in the ass*. Leland, can you not have quartermaster Ledbetter transferred to another post?"

Tension in the room was broken at a loud rapping on the door. Nora ruffled her skirts. "I swear, if it's Elmira, I may really lose my temper." She yanked the door open.

A young private said, "Telegram for Dr. Pope. I was instructed to deliver it to the colonel's quarters, ma'am."

Nora lifted her skirt in a polite curtsey. She

thanked the private. "I'll take it." She covered the distance in two steps to hand over the message.

All eyes were on the doctor as he opened the yellow envelope. "Eureka! The State Mental Hospital in Warm Springs has agreed to take the women and will have accommodations ready as soon as they arrive." He gathered his hat and thanked Nora for the refreshments and for her assistance. He waved the telegram in the air. "I'll send an immediate reply."

Pope stopped with his hand on the doorknob. "Sergeant Bohanan?" He smiled, then allowed the smile to fade. "The information you've imparted, as shocking and disgusting as it is, has given me great insight. In the future, I shall be more empathetic than judgmental."

Chapter Nine

The late September morning warmed, the air weighted with damp earth and horse scents, a welcomed respite from the extreme cold and snow. The sounds of children's happy shouts and laughter drew Ford away from his desk to look out the window.

Suffused with delight and longing, he stepped out to the porch to watch a game of stick ball. No clouds hindered the morning's light, and the sun's rays were bright and clean. He swept his gaze over Birdie, who wore an ugly brown-and-orange plaid tweed coat for warmth. The hem of Birdie's green dress exposed the tops of white socks and worn brogans. The frumpy castoffs did little to quell Ford's imagination of her figure. Her slightly disheveled hair had been brushed until it gleamed. She had pulled it high atop her head and secured the long length with a green ribbon. When the sun hit the red strands, it was like light igniting sparks of fire. It was a sight that caused his heart to lurch with admiration. He wanted to reach out and rub the silken texture between his fingers. The thought coupled with her laughter had the beat of his heart quickening.

As the ball rolled toward her, she blocked the youngster who tried to steal it for his team. A smartly aimed stick swatted the ball, knocking it toward where Ford stood watching. He stepped to the ground to trap it with the toe of his boot and to stop it from rolling under the porch.

"Perfectly *uncivilized,*" Elmira Ledbetter chortled. "A woman of her age frolicking about with skirts above her ankles like a...a...I don't know what," she made a fluttery motion with a pudgy hand as if swatting a mosquito, "and running around screaming at the top of their lungs. It's enough to give one heart palpitations."

"Like a what, Mrs. Ledbetter? Like a young woman experiencing freedom without fear of being flogged for wanting to give a group of homeless, half-starved children a little pleasure at playing stick ball?" Ford replied without regret.

Color suffused Elmira's cheeks. She retorted peevishly, "I do not appreciate your tone, Captain. I was merely stating my opinion, which I am entitled to."

He sighed heavily. "Begging your pardon, Mrs. Ledbetter." His upper lip curled. "It appears you have nothing better to do than carp on a sunny day perfect for play. Perhaps I might ask the quartermaster to assign you to latrine duty, since that's where your mind seems to be."

"Why, I never! My husband wouldn't dare!" She gathered her skirts and flounced toward the sutler's store.

Birdie raced across the yard to stand in front of Ford. Her hair gleamed like a tousled halo around her face. A dimple deepened in her cheek as she smiled. "Good morning, Thack-ry." And then she corrected herself. "Captain Thackery."

He met her gaze with an amused smile. "You've been practicing."

"Yes. I am practicing every day." She spoke in

halting English. She pointed to the object he held in his hands. "May I have the ball, please?"

He was awed by her eyes as they caught a shaft of the sunlight reflecting from his office window. For the moment they reminded him of dark green crystals. Despite the wickedly puckered scar that marred her face, he wondered if she knew the full extent of her beauty. With some difficulty he dragged his mind to full attention.

"You are quite beautiful, you know?"

She frowned up at him. "I do not know this word—beautiful." And then she laughed gaily as she stretched her hands forward. "The children...they wait."

He lightly caressed the tips of her fingers as he placed the ball in her outstretched palm. She lifted soft liquid eyes to his. Her brows gathered in confusion. As she gazed up at him, her moist lips parted in a disarming blend of innocence and invitation.

"Woman with Iron Fist, throw the ball and come finish the game with us," a boy of about ten called out.

Birdie answered in words that Ford didn't understand as she tossed the ball to the child. "Here, catch. I will return in a minute."

When she turned back to Ford, her eyes met his with the merest telltale twinkle. She was about to shift away from him when he said, "Will you do me the honor of allowing me to escort you to the dance Saturday night?"

She inclined her head slightly, her features alight with curiosity. "Speak simple words, please."

The creases at the corners of his eyes softened. "Go with me to the dance."

Birdie huffed an audible sigh. "If it pleases you."

Their eyes met for a charged moment. "I must go now."

A berry red curl had escaped from the ribbon atop her head to trail down the scarred curve of her neck. She looked more like a child than a woman who had given birth and had endured years of unspeakable cruelty. He reached out and the silky tendril entwined around his finger as if to ensnare him. She flinched and backed away, then turned to sprint toward the storehouse where the old ones remained housed.

He sighed, feeling a vague pang of disappointment.

****

Later, gathered in their new quarters, Birdie sat cross-legged. She leaned forward and unlaced the heavy boots, then kicked them from her feet. She stretched her legs forward and wiggled her toes. "I do not like these heavy shoes. They are too small for my feet and cramp my toes."

Ja'meena relaxed on a brocade chair. "I saw that prune-faced Mrs. Ledbetter talking to Captain Thackery. From their expressions it didn't appear that it was a happy conversation, and the captain didn't look nearly so handsome with his upper lip curled into a sneer."

"I do not think she likes me." Birdie fingered the scar on her face. "What means 'beautiful'?"

Ja'meena said smoothly, "Beautiful is like a field of yellow flowers, or a newborn foal, or a field of corn with silk tassels. Why do you ask?"

Birdie's cheeks flushed as she shrugged her shoulders. "It is a new word I have learned."

Esther's voice seemed to come from far away. "Sergeant Miller's Christian name is—Ansel. He has asked me to go to the dance." The faintest hint of lilt crept into her voice.

As a habit she had acquired when nervous, Birdie fingered the scar on her neck. "Captain Thackery asked me. I am afraid. I only know dance made for war, and dance made for breeding rights."

Beside her, Birdie heard the settee crack as Esther sat forward. She closed her eyes and smiled. "I remember when I married my first husband. We attended barn dances." She clasped her hands to her chest and sighed. "We whirled and twirled to the music until we were breathless." And then her eyes misted. "I had almost forgotten. I was very young."

"In calendar years I have not been captive as long as the two of you." Ja'meena pointed to her head. "In here, four years seems like an eternity." She unfolded her length from the stool. Patiently she explained about socials, parties, dancing, and food etiquette, and dancing in the white man's world was for pleasure, not war or breeding rights.

"I am certain Mrs. Culpepper will have beautiful gowns for us to wear. I always fixed my lady's hair with curls and bows." Ja'meena plumped the sides of her coal black hair and let out a boisterous laugh. "There isn't much I can do to make this mass of corkscrews pretty except put a bow in it." Her smile deepened. "It would make me happy if you allow me to fix your hair for the dance."

The moon's pearly light sifted through the curtain and the three sisters by circumstance squinted through the shadows when their singing and dancing was disturbed by a series of raps on the door.

Esther hastened to light a lamp while Ja'meena opened the door. "Mrs. Culpepper, good evening." She swung the door wide. "Please come in."

"Whose lovely voice was I hearing?"

"Ja'meena's. Her singing is *beautiful*." Birdie gushed inwardly as she used her new word.

Nora Culpepper laid an armful of dresses over the back of the settee. "I wish I could offer you brand-new gowns." She fluttered her hands. "The ladies' league collected several for you to try on, as we didn't know your sizes."

She held out a green gown. "Priscilla Avery is the sutler's daughter. She's about your size, Birdie."

Birdie touched the woman's arm. "Thank you, Mrs. Cul-pepper. I will go to this dance because Ja'meena has explained dancing is fun."

Nora looked amused as she patted Birdie's arm. "Then it is agreed. Captain Thackery, Sergeant Major Miller, and First Sergeant Bohanan are your escorts."

"Escorts?" Birdie sent Ja'meena a questioning glance.

Ja'meena explained in Nez Perce, "Escorts…men who…protect you."

Birdie nodded vigorously, and repeated in English, "Escorts…men who…protect you."

Birdie followed the older woman to the door and opened it. Before Nora walked outside, Birdie touched her arm. She took a moment to collect the words inside her head before she spoke. "The people, there," she pointed toward the storehouse, "they will come to the party, too?"

Nora fished a handkerchief from the cuff of her sleeve. She hesitated. "Oh, dear, I'm not sure I know how to answer." Her eyes beseeched Ja'meena's aid.

A warm smile crossed the Negro woman's face. "I

will try to explain."

"Beg pardon, Mrs. Culpepper. I brought these ladies chow: beef broth, roasted potatoes, and creamed chipped beef." The mess cook scooted around Nora to set the tray on the table. "You ladies can bring the dishes to the mess hall in the morning." He tipped his hat and left.

Nora said her goodnights and followed the aproned man into the chilled air.

Sitting around the table, the women filled bowls with a murky liquid. Birdie choked on her swallow. "It tastes like the inside of a dirty moccasin."

Laughter echoed around the room.

Birdie broke off a piece of roasted potato and plopped it into her mouth.

"Birdie..." Ja'meena's voice was soft. "If we are to live among civilized people, we must learn their ways. It is not polite to eat with our fingers." She stabbed a bite of potato with her fork.

"Yes. I will try harder to remember." Birdie said with a wistful smile.

"Don't worry. It will all come back to you. Isn't that right, Esther?"

Esther had taken a keen interest in using her fork to dig the last crumb of potato from its charred skin. "For me, it comes in drifts and then in waves. We must realize that Birdie was a child when taken. For her, remembering such things is like trying to rope a wisp of smoke."

"You are a wise woman, Esther."

"Ja'meena, why did Mrs. Culpepper not answer my question about the old ones coming to the party?"

Ja'meena pushed her empty plate away. She cut her

eyes toward Esther as if looking for help. Esther simply shrugged her shoulders as she reached for the coffeepot and refilled their cups.

"Come, let us sit by the stove. I need to warm my bones." When they were settled, Ja'meena said, "Birdie, when you were taken to the Pawnee camp, how were you treated?"

It was as if a dark cloud covered Birdie's face. Her anger was apparent as she bit out the words. "Because my skin was not of theirs, I was beaten. They kidnapped me, took me to their village. I thought because they had killed my mother and father that they wanted to be nice to me. They made me a slave. If I could not lift and carry the heavy loads, I was beaten. When I could not make anyone understand my words, I was beaten." She lifted the hem of her dress and wiped tears from her eyes.

"I'm so sorry, Birdie. The way you were treated is called *prejudice*. Mrs. Ledbetter is prejudiced. She is a mean, spiteful person who thinks unkindly of people who do not meet her ideal standards, and there are many others at the fort who are like her. It would be cruel to invite the old ones and the children to the party only to have them shamed. Do you understand?"

"To hate so much is never a good thing." Birdie's voice drifted off. "Yes, and it saddens my heart."

Chapter Ten

Chilling gusts accompanied by a glowering September sky buffeted soldiers and trappers, storekeepers, women and children, puckishly snatching cloaks, hats, bonnets, and neck wraps. Cheeks and noses were brightened to a reddish hue, and shivers came from those more lightly clad. For the most part, the fort's inhabitants lined the boardwalk in varying degrees of eagerness to see what kind of spectacle the women being deported to the asylum in Warm Springs would put on.

Dr. Pope nodded. Ford opened the infirmary's door and in a soft commanding tone, said, "Birdie, it's time."

Birdie walked outside, holding two slender hands, Emmaline, clutching the rag doll to her chest, and Nancy Cartwright, who gripped the gray woolen scarf close to hide her horribly burned face. Her dark eyes darted back and forth as if searching the crowd.

"Sending these used-up bags of bones to the madhouse is where they belong," a gruff voice in the crowd yelled out.

Birdie's green eyes turned in a blaze of fury and settled on a bearded trapper wearing a hat sewn from skunk pelts. She knew his kind, as they had often visited among the villages, trading whiskey for the privilege of slobbering over the women and forcing unwanted favors. She yelled out in Comanche, "You are nothing but a worm, crawling out of your dark, dank hole to eat the flesh of poor innocents! I pray Kangi the Crow pecks out your eyes."

The trapper barked, *"Bitch!"*

Seizing the man's arms, Sergeant Major Miller whisked him away from the scene.

Emmaline huddled against Birdie. In a moment of clarity, she said, "I am damaged beyond repair, Birdie. Thank you for caring."

She gave Emmaline an affectionate squeeze, then released her hand. "I hope you find the peace you deserve." And then Emmaline allowed Dr. Pope to assist her and Nancy Cartwright into the wagon.

At Ford's signal, Ja'meena followed, holding the hands of Lucy Nelson and Minnie Sudsbury. Nervous giggles beset Lucy. Minnie bared her teeth, slowly allowing Ja'meena to guide her toward the wagon.

As soon as Lucy and Minnie were settled, Esther led Patricia Sherman and Clara Butler from the infirmary. The icy glare in Clara's eyes and the hawking in her throat served as a warning. Esther cried out, "No, Clara. If you spit on anyone, I will slap you silly."

Clara gave a cool disdaining smile, the sort a naughty child might bestow on a scolding mother.

Shrill screeches from an unhappy baby set Patricia Sherman to screaming. She stood rigid, her fist clenched against terror-drained cheeks. She screamed wildly, "My children...my children!"

Birdie sprang forward and grabbed Clara before she could dart away while Esther wrapped her arms around Patricia in a bear hug. "There are no Indians, Patricia. It's okay. You are safe."

Patricia's shrill yelps set the wagon horses to rearing. The wagon lurched forward. The driver jerked on the reins to steady the animals as he crooned, "Whoa, there. Easy now."

Sternly, Colonel Culpepper commanded, "Quiet her down."

Dr. Pope reached for Patricia. Her eyes widened in horror, and her shrieks grew louder. "What in God's name set her off, Esther?"

"It was that baby's piercing cry. Poor Patricia, she lives with the frightening screams of her students inside her head."

Pope tried to go on, but the wails only increased. Suddenly, Esther's patience wore thin. She stepped back and slapped the woman, her left hand leaving an angry red blotch on her cheek. Patricia stopped screaming. She stood stiffly, her eyes fixed in terror, seeing nothing.

Esther's voice was shaky. "I'm sorry, Patricia." She gave the doctor a woeful look. "We can get her in the wagon now."

Jethro Pope nodded affirmatively.

Sniggers emitted from onlookers. Colonel Culpepper's voice boomed with authority, "Show's over. Troopers, get to your duty stations on the double. The rest of you go about your business."

The sun was trying to break through gray clouds when a trooper leading two horses joined the small farewell party. He stood holding the reins of the saddled mounts.

Colonel Culpepper extended his hand. "I'm skeptical about you leaving us without a doctor, Jethro."

Dr. Pope clasped the colonel's gloved hand. He smiled and cut a sideways glance. "The only emergencies I expect were just loaded in the wagon. Nora is as good a nurse as they come. As you well know, your wife has assisted me many times.

"Besides, it's necessary to keep the women as calm as possible for the next five days. Frankly, I don't trust anyone other than myself to see that they get proper dosages of valerian and are properly cared for along the way. Besides..." He patted the leather pouch slung over his shoulder. "I want to discuss their case histories with the chief of psychiatry and see what methods of treatment are available to them."

Nora Culpepper chided, "Jethro, why don't you just admit that you're curious to see the insides of the new hospital." She grew serious. "I do hope you're not thinking of leaving Fort Ellis. Why, I don't know what we'd do without you."

Jethro Pope strode to the side of the wagon. "Trooper, secure my horse to the tailgate. I've decided to ride on top for a while." Pope stepped on the toe rung and hauled himself up on the high seat next to the driver. He smiled down. "I'd never abandon my post. But, seriously, sometime in the future, I do plan to retire and enter private practice. By visiting the institution, let's basically say I'm exploring my options."

Birdie's voice was barely audible as she and Esther and Ja'meena stood in the middle of the yard and watched the covered ambulance rolling away from the fort. "That could be us instead of them."

****

From the center of the mantel, the cherrywood

captain's clock chimed the sixth hour, each chime ringing louder in Birdie's ear. The room was a myriad of candles and lanterns whose flames frolicked in jubilant accord with Colonel and Mrs. Culpepper's guests as they blended with the festive laughter of officers and their wives.

Birdie settled her hand deeper in the crook of Ford's arm. Bracing herself for the worst, she straightened her spine and smoothed the emerald green gown over the hooped skirt that covered layers of petticoats. Ja'meena had parted Birdie's rich russet hair down the middle and neatly coifed it at the nape of her neck, where she'd fastened it with a velvet green bow, the strands trailing down the back of the gown. A gift from Ford, a gold chain hung around her neck with a tiny gold sparrow, its wings spread as in flight, nestled at the full swell of her breasts.

Ford led her deeper into the room, introducing her to the lieutenants and their wives, and some of the bachelor officers. It seemed that everyone in the room ogled her, adding to her growing apprehension. She had the feeling she was less than welcome, and hoped her tight smile didn't look as artificial as it felt.

"Lieutenant Huxley, Miss Priscilla Avery, may I present Miss Birdie Mae Dix." Ford winked at Birdie. "Watch out, he's a charming fellow."

Priscilla offered a smug smile. "I never really liked that dress. I'd have tossed it in the trash a long time ago, but Mama wouldn't hear of it. Green simply doesn't suit my complexion." She toyed with a dangling curl and sighed. "Wouldn't you agree, Ford...darling?"

Birdie didn't understand all the words being hurled

at her. She surmised that the girl yapping her jaws like a magpie wasn't much older than herself and that from the arrogant tone and the self-righteous smile the words weren't complimentary. She glanced up at Ford. Puzzlement rested upon her brow. "What means this?"

"Oh, the poor darling." Priscilla extracted her arm from the lieutenant's and lifted her hand to dance nimble fingers down the gold buttons on Ford's blue dress jacket. "We simply must see to her education. To survive among respectable folk she cannot remain ignorant. Otherwise how will she ever snare a suitable husband? Of course, living among the savages could quite possibly limit the prospects of anyone other than..." she released a shudder, "those vermin-infested trappers and foul-mouthed whiskey drummers."

Ford clasped Priscilla's hand and pulled her close, a snapping chill in his voice when he spoke. For all who were watching, he gave an easy smile as he whispered, "Careful, Priscilla. There's more than one trooper who's tasted your fruits. Too much whiskey causes diarrhea of the mouth." He cocked a threatening eyebrow.

She pulled back, fanning the red spots on her cheeks. "Excuse me. I must speak to Mrs. Ledbetter." She cut simpering eyes toward the lieutenant. "Don't forget to save a dance for me, Huxie."

Lieutenant Huxley rolled his eyes before quirking a sly smirk. "Miss Dix is right handsome, Ford. Careful one of us bachelors doesn't try to steal her way."

At this comment, Birdie gripped Ford's arm tighter. She tensed, her heart lurching into an uneven rhythm. She was taken aback by Ford's hearty bark of laughter. "It's a compliment, Birdie. It's his way of saying that you are beautiful."

She heard the smile in his voice as she touched the tiny bird that hung at her throat. "I suppose you think I'm dimwitted not to know his meaning."

"You are anything but dimwitted. In fact, there's a rather overpowering honesty about you that I quite admire, Miss Birdie Mae Dix."

He led her to the refreshment table and poured two cups of punch. Their fingers met briefly as he handed her the cup. His touch seared her fingertips much the way an August sun scorched the earth.

The band struck up a lively tune. Before Birdie could protest, Lieutenant Huxley removed the cup she held and shoved it into Ford's hand.

Huxley's eyes glittered with mischief. He gave Birdie a courtly bow. "If you'll excuse us, Captain, I do believe this is our dance."

"B-but I don't know how." Birdie threw Ford a helpless glance.

Before Ford could protest, the lieutenant had grabbed Birdie's hand and whisked her into the reel, leading her down a line of clapping and hooting officers and wives. Ford watched her being passed from hand to hand, her cheeks growing pink with exertion, her frown blooming into full-blown laughter as she passed from Ansel Miller to Esther, then to Isaiah Bohanan, and to Ja'meena. Birdie tossed back her head, and kicked up her heels, her skirts sashaying back and forth in time with the music.

Her gaze ranged slowly around the room until it came to rest on Elmira Ledbetter and a group of busybodies from the ladies' league. The chocolate-brown gown with a voluminous skirt did not compliment the heavyset woman's figure. Birdie's mind ranged back to when she had first encountered the woman and the nasty remarks she had made about the *crazy* women. But she had worked to dismiss Elmira's poor attitude toward her and all of the captives.

She was struck with a strong aversion toward Elmira's booming laughter and arrogant attitude, and the women now in deep conversation sauntered casually to the refreshment table.

Birdie's intuitive sense informed her that these cold and calculating ladies were planning an attack. She stopped hearing the dance caller and instead heard the voice of a Comanche grandmother, *Woman with Iron Fist, never cry when you can fight. Sometimes a warrior must find a spot and make his stand, even if it turns out to be his last one.*

The music stopped and the lieutenant escorted her to where Ford stood. "For a gal that claimed she didn't know how to dance she sure kicked up her heels. I reckon war dances and whooping it up around Comanche campfires was good practice."

Ford's eyes narrowed. He swore beneath his breath before he said, his voice contemptuous, "Your words are unbecoming an officer and cruelly spoken, Lieutenant. It is apparent that you've had more than your share of the spiked punch. You will apologize to the lady and then take your leave."

The blood drained from Birdie's face, leaving it as pale as driven snow. She bit her lip, visibly composing herself.

"My, my, my. At least Lieutenant Huxley has the courage to say what many of us have on our minds." Elmira Ledbetter settled her hands on her waist. She puffed up like an enraged hen. "You can scrub the filth off these soiled doves, dress them in silk gowns, pretty up their hair, but it doesn't change the fact that they've wallowed with savages."

A scarecrow of a woman clad in black, sidled to stand beside Elmira. She spoke through snarling lips. "Can't trust 'em not to release the prisoners in the storehouse. Next thing you know, we'll be scalped in our sleep."

Other women's voices rang out. "They ain't fit to live among decent white folk. Send all three of 'em back where they belong—with the savages."

Grinding his teeth in vexation, Ford mangled several expletives. "You call yourselves *ladies*?" He laughed. "The Pawnee tattoo their captives. You ladies need to tattoo *hypocrite* across your foreheads. Captive women, white or from other tribes, don't know Monday from Sunday. All they know is seven days a week, twenty-four hours a day. Cooking is an activity that gives the women a little bit of a break from their usual drudgeries. You see, a woman's job is to serve, and after they've worked all day, they get to chew the fat out of buffalo hides to soften it so the men that have claimed them can have a new pair of moccasins."

His eyes flashed like the edge of crossed sabers.

Birdie stepped forward, her spine stiff with indignation. She spoke slowly to make sure her words were understood. "You people smile with your teeth, but it is your eyes that bite. You act as if I..." She spread her hand toward the startled faces of Esther and Ja'meena. "As if we are filth that will jump on you and not wash off."

A bloom of rosy color brightened her delicately

boned cheeks, setting off a spark of emerald fire in her eyes. She caught her breath in high-flying indignation. "English, the language of my white mother and father, I am learning every day." She reached out and grabbed Elmira Ledbetter's wrist. "If I cut your skin, what color do you bleed?"

Elmira answered with scorn as she yanked from Birdie's grip. "Any idiot knows blood is red."

In a surprisingly swift move, Birdie grabbed two cups and smacked them together. She lifted a shard of glass from the table and swiped it across her palm. She held her hand forward. "I, too, bleed red, Mrs. Ledbetter." And then she wiped her bloody palm across Elmira's chubby cheek.

For a moment Birdie was held frozen by the anger she saw blazing at her, and then she lifted her chin with an elegant air and dared a counterattack. She said with such gentle sarcasm that Ford winced, "Until our fate is decided, I will stay in the storehouse with those who do not judge me."

Although she wanted nothing more than to burst into tears and storm out of the room, she forced herself to turn and walk calmly out the door, her head held high.

Chapter Eleven

Clothed in hand-me-downs and wearing the ugly plaid coat, Birdie looped her arms over the corral's top rail and watched the newly purchased horses. She wanted to get away from the fort and the feeling that all eyes were watching her. A brown mongrel dog scooted under the corral's bottom rail, giving chase to a jackrabbit. Birdie grinned. The barking and the darting back and forth between the hoofed feet set off wild commotion. The young broncs acted like a bunch of excited children, running and kicking and biting in the cool morning air. As soon as the rabbit escaped, with the yapping dog giving chase, the horses settled down to find their own place in the enclosure.

Birdie placed both feet on the bottom rail and pulled herself to the top so she could sit. She spoke softly to the animals. "We are kindred spirits, my four-footed friends. My freedom was stolen. Your freedom was stolen. Those who captured me tried to break my spirit, just as the soldiers will try to break yours. You must accept it, as I have, because that is the way it is."

A blood bay gelding approached, stretching its long neck forward.

Dark brown eyes were wary and ready to flee.

Birdie offered her hand, palm open, to allow the horse to sniff, and to earn his trust. Inch by cautious inch, the young gelding moved forward and allowed

Birdie to caress his nose. She stroked the velvety pink flesh, feeling tears well in her eyes.

****

Ford shuffled through a thick packet of papers. His jaw worked in anger from the effects of last night's dance and the grief caused to Birdie and her friends. He tossed the papers back down on his desk. "Damn."

Too agitated to work, he buttoned his coat and grabbed his hat from the rack. Once outside, the chilled air cooled his agitation. His lips curled into a reluctant smile when he spotted Birdie perched on top of the corral fence and stroking the forehead of a half-tamed bronc.

Birdie's was the sort of beauty that needed no cosmetics to enhance it. She didn't need a fake beauty patch to draw attention to the plumpness of her kissable lips or rouge to heighten the natural roses in her cheeks.

Had the circumstances of her life been different, she might have been judged for superficial imperfections such as her nose a fraction too sharp or her jaw a shade too strong, but he would have condemned them as fools. He found her flaws as endearing as her spirit, especially the depth of green in her eyes, and the hair that reminded him of ripe raspberries.

Last night it was as if she had cast a seductive spell over him. And without trying she had mesmerized him with the misty glow of her eyes, the tantalizing way her lips parted when she'd taken a sip of punch. Her skin felt like silk beneath his fingertips, and he wondered if she was that soft all over. He'd wanted to savor the fragrant warmth of her sigh against his lips...

"Morning, Captain." A young private offered a

salute before passing by. Ford returned the courtesy, annoyed that his musing had been interrupted.

Swearing softly beneath his breath, he straightened. His uniform trousers had grown uncomfortably tight and his traitorous body was urging him forward. He stepped from the porch to the ground, returning salutes from subordinates.

He stalked toward her, kicking a stone out of his path.

"Hey, you, girlie, get down from there." A grizzled old corporal with bushy eyebrows yelled out.

"I am not going to steal them." Birdie's voice shook with anger.

"Listen, you, I said—"

Ford barreled forward. "As you were, Corporal. Saddle my horse and one for the lady."

The corporal saluted. "Yessir. What kind for her, sir?"

Ford could hear her breathing and see the angry rise and fall of her breasts. A warm current rippled over him. If the ache between his legs intensified, he wasn't sure how comfortable he'd feel sitting in a saddle. A slow smile spread across his face as Birdie looked down at him. "You do ride?"

Birdie raised her eyebrows. She pointed to the horse she had befriended. "The blood bay with the star. I will ride him."

The corporal gasped. "But, sir, ain't none of these broncs proper broke. I don't know if I can even get a saddle on him."

Ford looked into Birdie's bemused face. "Not today, Birdie. You'll like Gunpowder."

The corporal stared incredulous. "Gunpowder?

Beggin' pardon, he's a might spirited, sir."

"I'll take full responsibility."

The corporal stood at attention, his hand frozen in a salute.

"We don't have all day, Corporal."

"Oh, right, sir." The corporal spun on his heel and hustled to the stables, shouting, "Private Larson, saddle Captain Thackery's horse, and Gunpowder. On the double. We ain't got all day."

Ford reached up to help Birdie from her perch. Her smile robbed the breath from his lungs. The fire in her eyes heightened the desire to kiss her as it rose fast and fervent in his chest…and surprised the hell out of him.

She was so unlike Priscilla Avery, who had used every wile in the books to seduce him. He held an admiration for Birdie, who was shadow and mystery, enclosed in a cloud of sexuality, whereas Pricilla was conniving and deceitful. She had used her charms on him, and he'd almost fallen into her devious web and, on the cusp of proposing, had even purchased a wedding band. He harrumphed, thankful for the spewing of a slobbering drunk drummer who'd boasted of deliciousness between a certain sutler's daughter's legs. The man had winked, and in a comical gesture had mimicked turning a key between his lips.

Ford wanted to know more about Miss Birdie Mae Dix. A helluva lot more.

The corporal approached, holding the reins of two horses. "Here you are, Captain. Uh, ma'am, Gunpowder, he ain't been ridden in a while. Might be feeling a bit feisty."

Birdie's smile shot across like a radiant beam and speared the center of Ford's heart. "A Nez Perce appaloosa? He's beautiful."

Without waiting for assistance, she gathered the reins, grabbed the saddle horn, and like a bird in flight swooped into the saddle. The horse reared and pawed the air. Birdie chortled like a happy child.

"Corporal, go to the quartermaster and advise him that he is to write out a bill of sale in the name of Miss Birdie Mae Dix as the new owner of Gunpowder."

"Yessir."

Ford's smile widened as he gigged his prancing gelding forward. "He's a handful. Sure you can handle him?"

Birdie rolled her eyes and blew out a breath. "I'll race you."

****

The Bridger Mountains stood majestic in the background. Puffy little clouds tinged with pink drifted through a brightening sky.

A hollow feeling gave way to a vast array of emotions. Birdie's voice stayed steady, but underneath she had a strange hot yearning. "They are so close it feels like I could just reach out and touch them."

Ford relaxed on a boulder. He glanced up at the robin's-egg-blue sky, surprised at how high the sun had already risen. He slid from the boulder to gather a handful of stones. He skipped a stone across Hidden Lake. "Ah, but the clouds would melt through your fingers like the vapors they are."

Birdie joined him at the edge of the lake. She gave him a curious smile. "What means—vapors?"

This time the only thing he tossed was a cocky grin. "Vapors are smoke."

Ford simply gazed at her for a long moment before

saying softly, "Birdie, may I kiss you?"

She looked at him warily, shifting her glance from him to where the horses placidly grazed. "If it is like the slobbering on the mouth that the trappers do, then no!" She lifted her skirt ready to take flight.

"Wait." Ford caught her arm. He ached with a raw hunger that made him want to devour more than her pretty mouth. He crushed her against his body and cupped the back of her head with his hand, and brought his mouth down on hers, cutting off her protest in mid squeal. He hadn't anticipated that the softness of the mouth crushed beneath his would give him the taste of both heaven and hell. The flames only licked higher as she wrapped her free hand around the nape of his neck and clung on as if her life depended on it. She moaned her helpless pleasure into his mouth.

He slipped his hands inside the plaid coat and lightly wrapped them around her waist, pulling her closer. He felt the shiver wrack over her, and then she forcefully pushed him away. She sucked in air, trying to catch her breath. Her hand rose into a balled fist.

He hadn't missed her fear when he placed his hands around her waist. "I wouldn't hurt you, Birdie. You must believe me."

She touched her lips. Panic flashed in her eyes.

"I won't touch you again. I would not dream of dishonoring you." He motioned to the boulder. "Please, let's just talk."

She nodded, biting her lower lip. "What do you wish to talk about?"

Reining in his lustful thoughts, he answered honestly, "Tell me all you can remember about your capture. Even if you think it's not important."

Birdie shifted so that her back leaned against the massive rock.

She narrowed her deep green eyes and stared out at the snowcapped peaks of the Bridger Mountains. She crossed her arms and expelled a deep sigh, her face void of emotion as if shoving aside the deep reflections of her past.

"Papa worked in a factory. Someone told him about cheap land in the West. I remember we traveled in covered wagons with a lot of other people. One morning Mama woke me and said she was baking me a special cake, an upside-down cornmeal berry cake, because it was my fifth birthday. I was playing with my new sock doll and watching my brother. I think he was perhaps two years old because he was just walking without falling down.

"It was after breakfast and before supper when they came like chittering birds, whooping and hollering, their faces painted like devils. Mama screamed for Papa. She scooped my brother in her arms and told me to hide. There was so much blood." Birdie clasped her hands over her ears. "I can still hear the screams."

Ford reached out and she shrugged away from his touch.

"I didn't know for a long time that it was the Pawnee who raided the wagon train. I saw my Papa die. A warrior with a yellow-and-red-painted face rode off with my little brother. Another one grabbed me. Mama ran after him. I watched as a horse ran over her. I didn't see her get up."

"Birdie..." Ford had removed his hat and raked a hand through his hair.

"Please, let me tell it all without interrupting,

Loretta C. Rogers

because I never want to say it again." She grabbed the lapels of his coat. "Do you hear me...NEVER!"

He smoothed a stray strand of hair from her cheek and tucked it behind her ear. He admired her courage and perseverance. His heart reached out with sadness for Birdie's ordeal.

"Every time I would speak English the old women would take turns beating me with willow switches. My back, like most captive women's, is laced with scars from the many lashings we endured. One day I was too exhausted to work anymore. When an old woman came with the switch, I balled my hand into a fist and knocked her down, and then I took the switch and beat her." She drew a breath. "I think I was twelve, maybe thirteen when the Comanche raided the Pawnee village. I was captured.

"Killer of Bears was the principal chief. His girl child had died and his woman grieved. The girl had been a captive since a baby, so I became her replacement because the woman could not produce more children. My life was still difficult. The Comanche children hated me. A rattler was put in my bed. I was held down and burned with smoldering sticks. A child does not complain to the parent, even if it is not the true parent. To complain is to show weakness. My fist became my weapon."

Birdie continued in a firm voice. "One day a regal warrior came to the village. He brought twelve fine horses. It was his bride price. Killer of Bears accepted the horses, and I was given to Sacred Killer, son of Elk Who Runs, Chief of the Lakota nation. Sacred Killer was the warrior who sired my son. I was seventeen. I listened to the old women and learned how to keep from getting with child. Angered that I did not produce another child, Sacred Killer found ways to punish me. When my son was five, I refused to give Sacred Killer more breeding rights, and he threatened to take me to the fornicating lodge and to keep my son from me."

She stopped talking. Blood rose hot on her cheeks. "The Comanche raided our camp. Sacred Killer was struck down. I did not cut my hair or blacken my face, and I did not wail his name. I was glad the Comanche drew blood."

Fury tightened Birdie's jaw. "I would be a slave no more. I wrapped my son in a blanket and ran to the river. We hid inside a beaver dam. We traveled by night."

"Where were you going?" Ford asked.

She could only shake her head at his query. "Anywhere, nowhere, I needed...wanted to get away." She drew a sobering sigh. "Half-starved and exhausted, I thought it was a great day when Chief Looking Glass of the Nez Perce people found us. And then your scout Levi Two Feathers found us." She shrugged. "My papa's name was Thomas Dix, and my little brother was called Tommy. I don't remember how my mother was called. I was so young maybe I never knew her name."

"Birdie, do you remember where the wagon train was attacked?"

"The wagon master said he was following the Oregon Trail from Saint Louis...maybe Nebraska Territory...I'm not sure." She glanced down at the tiny gold sparrow that rested against her bodice. "Thank you for this gift. It gives me comfort, for the telling has sickened me. Now that you know all of my secrets, I wish to return to the fort."

Without waiting for a response, Birdie gathered her skirts and ran. She grabbed the appaloosa's reins and lithely sprang into the saddle, then kicked the gelding into a hard run.

Chapter Twelve

Birdie fretted. "I am sick of this place. We have traded one kind of prison for another. We are not white, we are not Indian, we are *ohanzee*—shadows." She waited patiently in line with the others for a turn to use the privy. "It's been almost a month. Surely Chief Joseph has crossed into Canada by now." She stared up at the purpling sky, her voice desolate. "Maybe he sent scouts and couldn't find us. Maybe the scout saw the bleaching bones and remnants of clothing on the trail and decided we had all died."

It was on the tip of Ja'meena's tongue to agree, but she didn't. She drew a deep breath. "I am black, and I, too, am *ohanzee*. It is up to Colonel Culpepper to decide our fate. My guess is he will send these people to a reservation. Only he knows where he might send us."

"I have heard evil talk about reservations." Esther's voice was indignant.

The privy door opened and a middle-aged woman stepped out, holding the hand of a mixed-blood child. Her eyes downcast, she trudged back to the storehouse.

Birdie grabbed the door. She waved a hand against the foul stench. "Are we no better off on a reservation than here?"

A cold wind drifted past, and Esther shivered and clutched the shawl tighter to her breast. "What happened yesterday? When you rode away with Captain Thackery you were happier than I've ever seen you, and then you rode in here like Kaga the demon was chasing you."

Resentment filled Birdie's reply. "Nothing important happened."

"It's not like you to be dishonest," Ja'meena chided.

Ford's handsome image sprang into Birdie's mind, and her heart beat a little faster. "I'm not interested in falling in love...ever." She fingered the little bird that hung around her neck. Her friend's accusing eyes squinting at her heightened discomfort. "Oh, all right, if you must know, he *kissed* me. He *kissed* me." She blinked and drew several breaths. "And worse I *liked* it." Her voice dropped to an astonished whisper. "What on earth is wrong with me?"

She didn't wait for an answer. Instead she scooted inside the outhouse and banged the door shut. She wanted to moan, weep in misery, or do something to find relief for the overwhelming yearning that swept through her. She had no business being attracted to him. She didn't want to be attracted to him. She needed to forget Ford Thackery and stay focused on leaving the fort and keeping her freedom.

Ja'meena leaned against the door and whispered loud enough so that only Birdie and Esther could hear. "Captain Thackery is a good man. You'd do well to latch on to him. Mm-hmm, I don't mind telling you that I've developed deep feelings for Isaiah, and I'm fair certain he has the same feelings for me. He just doesn't know it yet."

Esther laughed with lighthearted exuberance. "The

two of you are acting as addled as dazzled schoolgirls."

Ja'meena said, "You would reject the opportunity to love, to be protected and cared for, if Ansel Miller offered it to you?"

Birdie opened the door and stepped out. She inhaled deeply to clear the outhouse stench from her nostrils. "What would you do, Esther?"

Esther replied rather wistfully, "I want a home and family, but what man desires a woman who cannot produce children? Besides, Sergeant Major Miller is married to the cavalry. I seriously doubt he's interested in taking a wife."

A pause in their conversation allowed Birdie to think for a moment. As they strolled toward the storehouse in the waning light, she mused, "A warrior gives horses when he desires to buy a wife, does he not?" She skipped in front of Esther, reached out, and lifted the horse-head necklace that Ansel Miller had hand carved from a piece of dark ebony wood. She cocked an auburn eyebrow, a smug smile twitching on her lips. "I would say he's interested."

Esther gave a lame shrug and suddenly seemed flustered. A cloud moved away from the moon and the silvery light revealed a glow on her cheeks.

Silence prevailed between the three friends as they entered the storeroom and found their places among the other captives.

****

It was good to get away from the fort and the undercurrent of whispers whenever she passed a group of men or women. Esther smiled and gave her attention to a jackrabbit that scampered across their path. She decided to set her uneasy feelings aside and enjoy the day.

Sergeant Major Miller grinned as he held a wicker basket in one hand and his other hand at the small of Esther's back as he guided her some fifty yards from the fort and toward a grove of ponderosa pines. Someone had cleared a picnic area and had fashioned a long bench among the trees.

She sighed deeply, inhaling the crisp morning air. She felt suddenly foolish. She had no real business being here with this man. A laugh trembled in her throat as she pointed. "Two golden eagles! Look how they dip and soar on the wind. It is a good omen."

"Yes, ma'am, this is a special place."

"Do you come here often?"

As if he suddenly remembered his manners, he removed his cap and set it and the basket on the bench. "Only when time allows."

"Sergeant Major?"

"Yes, ma'am?"

"I would like it if you called me Esther."

He reddened. "Yes ma—uh—Esther. Fair enough, if you will call me Ansel."

"Ansel," she repeated. "It is a strong name." Esther sat. "It was nice of you to bring food. Did you make it?"

He snorted. "I'd be lyin' if I said so. I enlisted the aid of Mrs. Culpepper." His hand trembled as he opened the basket, and he couldn't seem to steady his fingers. "She said there were egg salad sandwiches, something called petty-fours, and a jug of water."

A smile flitted across Esther's lips. "I believe we are both a little edgy."

His ruddy hue deepened. "I'm a crusty ol' sergeant

set in my ways. I've fought in more campaigns than I care to remember, been wounded several times, and even had to cut a bullet out'n my leg, but I don't have much experience when it comes to courtin' a fine lady like you."

She blinked her surprise at his testament, and then her heart fluttered. *Fine lady.* The words caught in her throat.

She lifted two sandwiches from the basket and handed one to him. Her voice was quiet as she removed the wrapper and nibbled. "If I didn't say it before, I wish to thank you for the necklace. Did you carve it yourself?"

He looked down at the sandwich, the tips of his ears reddened. "It's a hobby my gran'pappy taught me when I was a li'l sprout." He filled his mouth with an oversized bite and choked on the swallow.

Esther jumped to his rescue by thumping him on the back. While he was still coughing, she uncapped the jug and offered a swig of water.

His eyes watered as he laughed. "I think you just saved me from chokin' to death."

She laughed too. "You were telling me about your whittling."

He cleared his throat several times, and managed to say, "Whittlin' gives me comfort. It helps me forget things that I don't rightly want to remember. Old ghosts, if you know what I mean."

Esther looked thoughtful. "In my other life, I used to grow beautiful flowers. Flowers make me happy." Quiet now, she stared out at the mountains. "Old ghosts...yes."

"I don't mean to pry, Esther. How did you come to

get captured? 'Course, it's none of my business and you don't have to tell me…you don't have to tell nobody."

The day was not cold, and yet she suddenly felt chilled to the bone and resisted the shivers that threatened to beset her. She glanced up and saw honest kindness in his brown eyes. "It is a long story. The dark and ugly details need not be told."

He nodded his understanding.

She tossed the partially eaten sandwich into the woods. "I had two husbands. The first I deeply loved. The other I prayed every day that death would take him. I was sixteen when I first married. We were happy. He bought flower seeds, and each year my garden would burst with colors of the rainbow. After three years I had not yet birthed a child. I saw the sadness in his eyes. I was sad, too. I think we began to drift apart. One day when he was plowing, a fierce storm came. No rain, only thousands of fingers of lightning. That night I buried him and the mule right where they lay." She drew a shuddering breath.

"When I was twenty, I went to a tent meeting. The preacher man walked right down the aisle and placed his hand on my shoulder. Handsome and regal and a cleft chin, he could sweet talk the devil. I was lonely and foolish enough to believe he was a righteous man. It wasn't until after we married that he introduced me to his sons, ages thirteen and eleven, and meaner than any wolverine. At the meetings he put on a show pretending to heal one of the boys of his lameness, and at other times, the older boy pretended to be a deaf mute…" Her laugh was sardonic. "And people gave Oren Bullard their hard-earned money because they, too, fell prey to his charm. We traveled by covered wagon from town to town, and sometimes when a clever person figured out they were being flimflammed, we were run out with threats of being tarred and feathered.

"We were camped near some nameless shambles of a town that sprang up around a gold mine that had petered out. A wife with a black eye and a split lip isn't good for business. I got used to the beatings long before the Hunkpapa captured me. Anyhow, I was asleep in the wagon when they came. A blanket was thrown over my head. All I could hear were gunshots and screams. The rest you know."

She rose to stand before him. "I am no longer young. As best as I can remember, I am near forty-five years old." Her eyes lowered, she scrubbed a circle in the dirt with the toe of her boot. "You are a good man, Ansel Miller. I am not a proper woman for a good man."

She felt bloodless and withered. "The magic in this place is for fools." She lifted her skirt to flee. Ansel caught her by the elbow.

"Esther?"

"Yes." Turning, she saw no condemnation in his eyes.

"I'm not much to look at, what with a pot belly and a bald spot on my head. In a few months I'll see fifty years. I'd like for you to know that these past few weeks you've made me feel more alive than..." He scrubbed the side of his cheek. "Than since I can remember."

She wasn't sure she had caught his meaning. There was no commitment between them. She told herself that's the way she wanted it. A dull ache stabbed the center of her heart. That's the way it *had* to be. As soon as the colonel heard from the big chief in Washington, she would leave with the other captives. All the more reason she shouldn't be snatching time with him and adding to memories that would continue to haunt her for the rest of her years.

She shirked away from him and ran. Tears blurred her vision, blinding her as she raced toward the fort. Just as she reached the middle of the yard, a stone flew from nowhere and struck her between the shoulder blades. She gasped. The pain knocked her to her knees.

Ansel let loose the picnic basket. He raced as fast as his bandy legs would carry him. "Stay down, Esther."

She had already begun to stand when another stone glanced off the side of her head. Blood trickled from the wound.

He whirled about. "See here!" Ansel bellowed. He ranged the perimeter, unable to spot the culprit. Without comment, he swept Esther into his arms and hurried to the infirmary.

"I'm sorry, Esther, sorry as I can be that some no-good kid with a slingshot hurt you. I'll wring his dang neck when I find 'im." His voice was low and surly.

She quickly gained her composure. "Every day Elmira Ledbetter and her so-called posse, and the storekeepers, the children, and some of the soldiers speak eloquently with their silent condemnations."

She couldn't help inhaling the musky scent of his aftershave lotion mingled with his manly odor. An irresistible urge seized her to trace her fingers along the strong edges of his jawline.

"There's no need for you to carry me, Ansel. I can walk."

106

"A head injury might cause you to faint if you exert yourself." He persisted, "Besides, you might need stitches." He gave her a long look that spurred her heartbeat until she was lightheaded not from the injury but from a long-suppressed need to be loved, truly loved.

The infirmary door banged open. Nora Culpepper looked up from her crocheting, setting it aside. Irritation laced her voice. "What happened—or should I say, who did this?"

She walked to the medicine cabinet and removed a bottle of alcohol, a cotton wad, tincture of iodine, and gauze for a bandage. "Set her on the examination table, Sergeant Major."

Esther shrugged as she settled on the edge of the wooden table. "It does not matter. Those who hate will always hate."

She sighed. She would miss Sergeant Major Ansel Miller and Nora Culpepper a lot more than she wanted to admit.

Chapter Thirteen

The morning was warmer than usual for early October. Nora Culpepper, holding the hem of her simple gown, marched across the parade ground, head held high. At the storehouse door she pivoted and smiled at the plump woman standing on a set of wide porch steps. "Lovely morning isn't it, Elmira?" *Meddling old fool.* "I've invited the ladies for morning tea. Care to join us?"

Elmira frowned her disapproval but nonetheless, as if she were a curious spectator, remained where she stood.

The storehouse door creaked opened. "We've been watching for you." Birdie's voice was timid as she stepped outside. "Umm, Nora, Maria Alvarez's little girl has a bad cough and a fever. We've been up most of the night caring for the child." Birdie's eyes beseeched the colonel's wife. "Maria is a captive from Texas. The comancheros raided her village. She has been traded many times since. Her life has not been good. She speaks only Spanish and Pawnee. Please, Nora, I think she was once a lady from a rich family. Let Maria enjoy tea. I will stay and tend the child, and Esther can translate. Okay?"

Nora reached out and clasped Birdie's knotted fist. "Of course, I completely understand. It's so good of you to want to give this poor woman a little bit of pleasure."

Birdie's gaze strayed to where Elmira Ledbetter stood, watching through a slitted gaze. Birdie shielded her eyes from the sun. "The fat one watches like a vulture waiting for death to come so she can pick our bones." She squared her shoulders and sighed. "Why does she hate us so much?"

Nora smiled slightly, her tone serious. "One day Elmira Ledbetter will need to eat a big slice of humble pie, Birdie. When she does I hope she chokes on it."

Birdie quietly surveyed her friend, allowing the words to sift through her brain. "Of course...I do not know what you mean, but...never mind." She shrugged. "I will get the others."

She beckoned inside the open door. "Come, Nora is waiting." In Pawnee she said to Maria, "Do not worry about your little one. Go. Enjoy. Nora is a friend."

Maria managed to subdue her tears. Birdie knew the fear and self-doubt that churned inside the Mexican woman. "Esther will translate for you." She made a shooing motion. "Go, and do not be afraid of the fat pig across the street. Nora says she needs to eat humble pie."

Maria Alvarez covered her mouth to hide the timid giggle. "Humble pie is not a food. I will explain later."

Nora linked arms with Esther and Ja'meena, and Maria held tight to Esther's hand. An hour later, a very pleased Nora opened the parlor door. Overhead the clouds writhed by with the promise of a wintry wind. At the corral frisky bay geldings, their coats growing thicker for the oncoming winter, snorted and kicked up their heels.

Nora thanked the ladies for joining her, and then

winked at Ja'meena. "Don't forget. This evening at four o'clock. He'll be waiting."

Suddenly, with only an increase in wind speed, the sky became gray and bloated. "Rain or snow, wild horses couldn't keep me away," Ja'meena promised.

Nora's gaze swept over to Maria. "Esther, tell her to bring the child to the infirmary. I'll meet both of you there."

****

Promptly at four in the afternoon Ja'meena stood at the top of the steps that led to Colonel Culpepper's living quarters. She took a moment to straighten the white collar of her brown gingham frock, then lifted her hand and tapped at the door.

Nora greeted her with a smile. "I feel as if I'm part of a secret conspiracy. It's so exciting." She beckoned to Ja'meena to follow. At the rear entrance she opened the door and leaned out. "Oh, there you are."

Isaiah stood outside. "You are a good friend, Miz Culpepper, ma'am, he'pin' us out like this. That Miz Ledbetter, she fo' sure do like to gossip."

A moment of darkness hung on Ja'meena's brow. It annoyed her that the label "captive" and "slave" and *worse* had been attached to her simply because of her circumstance. She guffawed. "Actually, I should have marched right up and knocked on Isaiah's door. That would surely set those ol' biddies' tongues a-wagging."

Nora patted Ja'meena's shoulder and chuckled.

Isaiah extended the crook of his arm. "My place is two doors down." He doffed his cap and bid Nora good evening. "I'll escort her back to the sto' house, Miz Nora."

A short few steps led to a back porch with two

rocking chairs that faced the mountains. A small table sat between the two rockers, and a glass jar filled with water held a bouquet of wild flowers. "I picked 'em fresh 'bout an hour ago."

Ja'meena lifted the jar and inhaled the sweet aroma. "They remind me of springtime in Charleston."

Isaiah laid a quilt across Ja'meena's lap. "Don't want you catchin' a chill. Now you jes' wait right here. I got fresh coffee…good 'n hot, and got the mess cook to bake up some cookies, too."

He disappeared for a split second and returned with a tray holding a porcelain coffeepot, steam spiraling up the spout, two delicate cups with saucers, and a plate of molasses cookies. He wore a sheepish grin. "Miz Nora gave me loan of her china. She said it came all the way from England."

"I think she's the only honest woman at the fort." Ja'meena forced herself to relax in the rocker. She steadied the cup and saucer on her lap, her eyes downcast, watching the breeze rustle around the folds of her dress. She listened, first to the deep sigh he expelled, then to his softly spoken words.

"Is yo' from the south, Miz Ja'meena? I do believe yo' has a drawl."

"You are quite astute, Isaiah. Yes, until four years ago, I lived my entire life in Charleston, South Carolina." She pressed her lips into a frown. "Life was beautiful and so simple before the war and the damned thieving carpetbaggers that came afterward."

He chuckled. "I do likes a woman who ain't afraid to speak her mind." His hand went out and touched her arm. She flinched. He said softly, "I would never hurt you." And then as if trying to lighten the mood, he said,

111

"By the time I was thirteen, I determined that walkin' behind the ass-end of a mule and pushin' a plow wasn't for me. I kissed my mam g'bye and ran off. Jes' a dumb kid is what I was. Only been back to Mississippi onct, and that was at her funeral, long time ago."

Her fingers began tracing the outline of the rose pendant he'd given her the night of the dance. "Were you a slave, Isaiah?"

"There's all kinds of slavery. I reckoned you'd know 'bout that." His features relaxed into a thoughtful cast. "I don't mean to sound offish. Yas, my folks and me were slaves, and the massah was tough. He 'spected a good day's work, but he weren't cruel."

His hand gently covered hers. This time she didn't flinch. "If'n it's not too painful, tell me 'bout South Carolina and how you come to get captured."

Her hand lifted to cover the brooch at her neck. The rush of thoughts flooding her brain made her dizzy enough to faint. She had done her daily chores with childlike indifference, had assisted her mama with the midwifing, helping with the difficult deliveries at the farm hands' quarters, and had beamed with pride each time a tiny face was brought into the world.

"Ja'meena, if it's too difficult for yo', I understand."

Shaking herself, she held out the cup for a refill, hoping to drive away the painful remembrances. "Most of the memories are sweet. A little black kinky-headed girl was born on the same night as a blonde, blue-eyed baby girl. Her mama named her Charlotte Rae. My mama named me Ja'meena. Since we lived and worked on the Pickett Plantation, most of the folks took Pickett as their last name.

"Charlotte was the fifth child of Mr. and Mrs. Pickett, and the only girl. By the time Charlotte was born, Mrs. Pickett was well past her prime. She was still fair to look upon, but nearing fifty. Something went wrong in the womb, and Charlotte was born with one leg shorter than the other."

The cool October evening wind stung Ja'meena's cheeks, and only then did she realize the moisture sheening in her tawny eyes as memories of her mother and Charlotte came to her. She lifted the edge of the quilt and dabbed at the tears.

"Mrs. Pickett's health declined, and my mama was brought to stay in the house as her caretaker. I, on the other hand, grew up scampering about on the wide veranda, being tutored right along with Charlotte, even learning to play the piano, and spending many happy hours sharing confidences with her."

She cleared her throat. "Even though I was born free, on my twenty-first birthday, Charlotte insisted that legal papers be drawn and filed in the recorder's office that officially stated that I was a free woman. She was quite intuitive, my Charlotte."

Isaiah listened, his face a study of surprise and awe.

"Time passed, and at the age of thirty, Charlotte was known as Charleston's wealthiest spinster. Oh, she had her fair share of suitors." Ja'meena grunted in annoyance. "She was smart enough to know that they weren't interested in a gimpy wife, only her money and the prestige that came with it."

"Long before the war, Charlotte had married Mr. Robert Alexander, a banker from Virginia. He didn't care one whit about her crippled leg. He doted on her.

Robert took over most of the duties of running the plantation, and he honored old Mr. Pickett's rule that all the darkies were paid a fair wage. Mr. Pickett didn't hold with slavery."

She swallowed back the sob in her throat. "You know about the cruelties of war, so specifics aren't important. One night the damned Yankees came. The big house with its fine Doric columns, all the outbuildings, and the crops were set afire, and Mr. Pickett's stable of fine thoroughbreds stolen. Mrs. Pickett, being feeble in both mind and body, was trapped in the second-story bedroom. Mr. Pickett died trying to save her." This time the sob loosed itself.

"Ain't no need to fret yo'self any more with details, Ja'meena. 'Tain't none of my business."

She coaxed a watery smile. "Please, let me finish."

He simply nodded.

"After the war was declared officially over, the carpetbaggers swooped in like a horde of hungry locusts. Robert sold everything that hadn't been destroyed and bought passage on a wagon train. He said we were going to San Francisco. Charlotte was ill, and he wanted to travel by rail." She shifted her shoulders. "He didn't have enough money for tickets. I offered to stay behind, but even so, he still didn't have enough, and he insisted that Charlotte needed me.

"We were nearly to Colorado when Charlotte's consumption grew worse. The wagon master said we had to leave the train. The folks were nice enough, sharing food and water to last until Charlotte got well. If she hadn't been so sick, I think being alone on the vast plains would have frightened me more than it did. It was the end of the fifth day when Charlotte drew her last breath. We had finished burying her and were placing the last stone on her grave when they came whooping like a bunch of crazed banshees. Robert opened his arms wide and faced them. Devastated over losing the love of his life, I don't think he felt the arrow that pierced his heart.

"The wagon was set afire. To this day I believe that being black and having kinky hair is what saved me from slaughter. If there is a hell on earth, I've lived it." Lifting her gaze, she saw the sheen in Isaiah's ebony eyes. "Every day since, I've wished that an arrow had taken my life, too." This time the tears flowed uncontrollably.

Isaiah lifted her from the chair and set her on his lap, where he cradled her like a hurt child. He crooned, "Anybody ever tries to hurt you again, they'll have to step over me first."

"What's to happen to us, Isaiah? I and the others had hoped Chief Joseph would send scouts to find us once he crossed into Canada. He was good and treated all people well. We are here and hated, though we have committed no crime." A sob shuddered through her. "We have no family, no home, and no money, even if we did have a place to go."

His eyebrows gathered in a perplexed frown. "Don't you fret yo'self. Everything's gonna be jes' fine."

Chapter Fourteen

"Colonel Culpepper sent for me?"

The duty officer looked up from his paperwork and scowled. "Yessir, Captain Thackery, and he's in a foul mood."

Ford nodded rigidly. He rapped on the door.

"Enter," Colonel Culpepper commanded.

As though he had read the colonel's mind, Ford removed his hat and sat without a word.

The colonel shook his gray-streaked hair, then glanced up from the two telegrams flattened out on top of his desk.

He walked from behind his desk to pace, slapping his hands together behind his back before he reached out and snatched the telegrams and slapped them against the palm of his hand. "What the hell is going on in Washington that the Bureau of Indian Affairs can't take five minutes to give me a reply?"

He tossed the yellow papers on his desk. His face drawn into a frown, he placed his hands behind his back again and paced. "I don't know how much clearer I can make it that we have a situation here. Hell, yes, I know we'll send those poor devils to a reservation, but where, which one? Answer me that! Fort Ellis is not a luxury resort. For crissake, we can't keep these people here forever." He swore beneath his breath and continued his rant. "And the other women..." He searched for an appropriate word to describe them and didn't find one.

The volume of his voice continued to escalate. "Mrs. Bullard was attacked for no reason. One of the children is sick with a fever, and now someone is spreading rumors that we have cholera at the fort." He slapped his fist against the palm of his hand. "It's about time Jethro Pope returned from Warm Springs. I need him to squelch this cholera rumor immediately."

Nora Culpepper opened the door that separated their living quarters from his office. Her voice was hushed but firm. "Leland! If can hear you through the walls, and so can everyone else. You'll give yourself apoplexy if you don't calm down," she chided gently. "Although I don't blame you. I believe you'd get more cooperation from a snail than you're getting from Washington." Nora shut the door and seated herself. "Of course, that's only my opinion."

Ford stood to greet Nora. "Good morning, ma'am. How is the child?"

Nora tsked and motioned for him to sit. "Sweet little girl. Her name is Rosario. She is severely congested from the croup and is having trouble breathing. I agree with Leland about Jethro's returning. I do well with minor cuts and such. However, I'm not trained in pharmacology and have no idea which medicine is best for the girl. I did make up a batch of whiskey and honey to ease the cough and help her sleep. And prayer helps. I pray it's enough."

A little voice warned Ford not to respond too hotly. He worked to quell his own silent rage. "Whatever you're doing is a hundred percent better than what a tribal medicine man could do." He rubbed one hand over his chin and redirected the conversation. "We believe it was Mrs. Ledbetter's son who attacked Esther…Mrs. Bullard." He shrugged. "Proving it is another thing because every boy at the fort under the age of fourteen owns a slingshot."

"Earl is fifteen, and I'll bet he still has a slingshot. I wouldn't put it past the boy to feed off his mother's antagonism. What I don't understand is why Quartermaster Ledbetter doesn't act like a man instead of a spineless worm and take his wife and son to task. The boy is known to be a bully. Can't you do something, Leland?" Nora asked.

Ford's teeth clenched. Anger simmered in his low voice. "I'm as angry as you, Colonel, that Washington is dragging its feet. As far as Earl Ledbetter, if it's proven he's the one who used the slingshot on Esther, I will gladly apply the lash to his back."

A sharp rap against the door broke the tension building inside the office. The duty officer burst through the opening. His young high-pitched voice squeaked with excitement. "Beg pardon, Colonel…Captain, there's a rider coming. His horse is lathered with sweat, and flaggin'."

Ford grabbed the hat from his knee and situated it on his head. He sprinted through the door and outside in time to see the sergeant major and first sergeant galloping full speed toward the faltering horse and rider.

Colonel Culpepper stood next to Ford. He groused, "If he wasn't on official duty, I'd have Jethro Pope court-martialed for dereliction of duty."

Nora stood next to her husband and as straight as any soldier. Under her breath she tried to keep the smugness from her voice. "Don't forget, you signed his official leave request. He should return in a day or two. Patience, Leland, patience."

Ford shielded his eyes. "Sergeant Major Miller has helped the rider from his horse and is assisting him onto First Sergeant Bohanan's mount." He continued his report with, "First Sergeant Bohanan is leading the exhausted animal in."

"Can you make out his attire?" The colonel wanted to know.

Ford took a couple of steps forward. "From this distance it's difficult to tell." He squinted. "I'm fair certain he's in uniform, sir."

Culpepper commanded, "Nora, get to the infirmary. We'll bring him there."

The colonel, too, shielded his eyes. He spoke to the officer of the day, who stood next to him. "Have the mess cook prepare a light meal and coffee. Bring it to the hospital." Before the duty officer spun on his heel to obey, Culpepper said, "And bring a bottle of whiskey."

As word spread about the rider, curious faces began to appear.

****

Birdie reached up to drape another dress over the corral's top rail. A shy sun peeked behind gray clouds. Birdie was thankful for the opportunity to wash a few clothes and blankets.

A toothless Nez Perce man ambled next to her and asked, "Woman with Iron Fist, what is happening that stirs the white-eyes like angry ants?"

She made a sweeping glance across the dirt yard and listened to the hurried footsteps of soldiers called to attention.

"I do not know, old one. It must be important

119

because the head chief rarely leaves his office, and now he waits with Captain Thackery." Her heart pounded faster as she gazed at Ford's broad shoulders and recalled his warm smile, his soft kiss… She sighed heavily, finding no regret in avoiding Ford, or her unwise fascination with him. She had pondered the best solution for not falling in love with Ford and kept circling back to the one reasonable answer—she had to avoid him as much as possible.

A sharp pain jabbed her chest. Birdie's shoulders slumped. So why did her heart keep protesting that one rational thing?

Footsteps resounded on the parade yard. A door banged and excited voices hummed. As soon as she spotted the sergeant major leading a horse with a trooper slumped forward in the saddle, her pulse pounded with a growing trepidation. "Old one, this rider has traveled far and nearly ridden his horse into the ground. Perhaps he carries our fate to the fort's head chief."

The toothless man nodded. Crows' feet were etched at the corners of keen brown eyes that looked as if they had seen plenty of hardships. "We are timeworn and useless. Do you think they will kill us?"

Birdie squared her shoulders. The question did not surprise her. "I do not. I have heard talk of sending us to a reservation."

The aged warrior harrumphed. "Not you, Woman with Iron Fist. You are not of us." He hugged the blanket closer to his withered body. "Wherever they send us, I hope it is warm."

His barb stabbed Birdie deeply. She answered in a soft monotone, "I think I belong nowhere."

Esther and Ja'meena joined Birdie. Esther turned a questioning frown toward Birdie.

Three vultures circled overhead. Clouds gathered behind Bridger Mountains. The distant peaks were capped in snow. Birdie lifted her eyes to the scavengers. A sense of foreboding filled her.

"Do you feel it?" Birdie's voice quivered. "Our fated-ness?"

The women joined hands. Esther said, "No matter what message the rider brings, we are sisters."

Ja'meena agreed. "Yes, sisters."

They watched in a vortex of silence as the sergeant major halted the horses. He tossed the reins to a trooper, then ordered, "As soon as First Sergeant Bohanan arrives, tend to that poor hoss he's leadin' in. And I don't mean jest turn 'im out in the corral. Animal's prob'ly bone dry. You know the drill, Private. Not too much water till he's properly cooled down, same with the oats."

The trooper saluted his acknowledgement as he held the reins of both horses.

Ansel Miller dismounted and assisted Ford with the rider. Ford said, "Did he say anything?"

"Yessir, Cap'n. He could barely squeak out the words. All I could make out was your name, sir." Ansel cast a look at the colonel. "I expect he has a message of sorts for you, Colonel."

"Captain, get him to the hospital. As soon as he's capable, we'll get our answers. Good job, Sergeant Major." Colonel Culpepper saluted, turned on his heel, and headed for the infirmary.

Ford ordered, "Privates Darby and Booth, get this man to the hospital."

121

****

Ford stood in the middle of the slushy gray yard waiting as First Sergeant Bohanan continued toward the fort, leading the sweat-lathered horse. He held an admiration for the man and his gentle caring nature for all things living, and he was more dependable than most—the kind of man you'd want next to you in a battle.

He noted the pathetic contrast between the neat row of log cabins known as officers' row, and the barracks that housed the enlisted men, and the humble but sturdy converted storehouse that lodged the captives. He was in a devil of a mood when Birdie caught his attention. She had draped a wet quilt across the corral rail. She wiped her hands down her slim hips as she turned. Time seemed suspended into endless moments of breathless anticipation as their eyes locked. A strong surge of lust swept through him, heating his blood and surprising the hell out of him. Immediate lust wasn't his style. Her strawberry-red tresses were pulled back in a severe style that emphasized her high cheekbones and long slender neck. Not even the scar on her cheek that traced down her neck marred her beauty. The morning sun's glow almost made her seem ethereal.

Her gaze was bold and smoldering. She was an intriguing mixture of sensuality and freshness, and scorching desire. Although a slight distance separated them, it felt as if she were only inches from him, and the yard seemed to sizzle with their combined heat.

He started at the first sergeant's softly voiced question. "Cap'n...yo' a'right, sir? 'Pears yo' is a thousand miles away."

Ford looked into Bohanan's coal black eyes. "Just thinking, First Sergeant," he replied after a moment, turning his gaze away from Birdie.

Bohanan cut his eyes to where Birdie stood. His lips twitched with humor. "Yessuh, Cap'n, jes' thinkin'."

A trooper collected the reins from Bohanan. "I'll take good care of him, First Sergeant. If I don't, Sergeant Major Miller will have my hide." He sauntered off leading the exhausted horse.

Still thinking about Birdie, Ford was certain she wanted him as much as he desired her. He smiled to himself. Winning her trust would be like trying to pull hen's teeth.

Chapter Fifteen

It was almost four o' clock. The sun would set in another hour and another long night would begin at Ft. Ellis. With the mystery of the dispatch rider's message about to be disclosed, Ford was as anxious as the other officers seated in the colonel's office.

Moments later, the officer of the day arrived with a large pot of coffee and a tray of mugs. He set them on a side table and left. Colonel Culpepper entered. All the men immediately stood at attention. "As you were," he commanded, taking a seat behind his desk.

Ford rubbed the knot of nerves at the back of his neck. His eyes flicked briefly to the pouch in the colonel's hand. By the look on the colonel's face, something big was about to happen.

Culpepper removed a letter from the leather wallet. His solemn expression evoked attention. Without a word of explanation, he unfolded the letter and read matter-of-factly, *"Friday, 5 October 1877, Chief Joseph and his band, the Nez Perce, have surrendered approximately forty miles shy of the Canadian border. The frigid weather, dwindling supplies, and endless miles of merciless terrain have taken their toll. Having seen his warriors reduced to just eighty-seven fighting men, having weathered the loss of his own brother, Olikut, and having seen many of the women and children near starvation, he surrendered in the Bear*

Paw Mountains. It is cold, and they have no blankets and no food. The little children are freezing to death. The defeat of the Nez Perce is a victory without pleasure. The day of the great warriors has come to an end.

Medical aid, ammunition, food, blankets, and a relief company is needed at the earliest. My own men are exhausted, starving, and ailing. Further, advise Washington that Chief Joseph has laid down his weapons and promised to fight no more. I will contain Chief Joseph and his people until orders are received on where to proceed.

"It's signed, General Nelson A. Miles." Without ceremony, Colonel Culpepper laid the missive on the desk. "I have already telegraphed President Hayes of this defeat." He seemed lost in thought for a moment. His eyes suddenly cut to Ford.

"Captain Thackery, choose your men and make ready for departure in no less than twenty-four hours, sooner if possible. As soon as word is received from Washington…"

A sharp rap sounded and the duty officer opened the door. "Sir." He thrust the telegram forward. At the colonel's nod, he spun on his heel and exited the room.

Ford thought he'd never seen the colonel's eyes looking so intense and dark. Deep lines had carved into his brow.

Colonel Culpepper met the expectant gazes. "Gentlemen…" He read the telegram out loud. "*Joseph and his Nez Perce are to be escorted to the railhead in Livingston, Montana, and shipped to Fort Leavenworth, Kansas, where they will be held as prisoners of war for the duration of their lives. Rutherford B. Hayes,*

President US."

Culpepper said, "We're off record. At ease, all of you. Ford, speak your mind."

Ford rose, arching his back to relieve the tension gnawing at him. He exchanged knowing glances with the two sergeants. "Fort Leavenworth is brutal. It's a hellhole. It's rife with malaria and other diseases. Most of them may not survive the long walk in inclement weather to Livingston, nor the train trip. Those who do..." Ford gritted his teeth. "Those who do..." His voice rose. "I'd heard President Hayes was a fair-minded man. Apparently not!"

"Beggin' pardon, suh." Isaiah dared a look at Ford's face and then to the colonel. "What 'bout the people in the sto' house?"

For a quick second, Ford was relieved that Isaiah had asked the question. "Yes, sir, we're specifically concerned about the women who aren't Indian."

The colonel stumbled for an answer. "I know you're concerned about the Misses Dix, Bullard, and Pickett. Until I receive detailed orders, all of the captives will remain here." He opened his hands wide to indicate his frustration. "It's the only answer I can give you."

Ford frowned with worry. "Permission to be excused, sir? It's better if we..." He indicated the two sergeants. "If we break the news to the women before rumors begin to fly."

"Yes, of course, we wouldn't want an unnecessary panic on our hands."

Moments later, Ford, Ansel, and Isaiah emerged from the colonel's office. Ford noticed at once the sun in its slow, late afternoon descent. A freezing wind whipped around them. Flurries of white flakes drifted from the leaden sky. Followed by the others, Ford moved quickly toward the storehouse.

Ford shook his head knowingly. "Tonight is the best opportunity to spend with the ladies. Take as much time as you need. However, be ready before morning roll call to prepare for a butt-busting trip to General Miles' location."

Ansel Miller moved in step with Ford and Isaiah. "How long you think we'll be out on maneuvers, sir? I'm sure the women will want to know."

Ford did a quick mental calculation. "We can't make good time hauling wagons, and allowing for snow, it'll be seven days to Bear Paw Mountains. Depending on the shape General Miles' men are in, and the Nez Perce, too, we can figure another seven days to the railhead at Livingston. We'll need to bring the wagons back once we leave Miles." His voice was deep and firm. "Near a month is my best guess."

A strange stillness suddenly settled upon the evening. Ford lifted his hand and rapped on the storehouse door. A wrinkled face greeted him. The woman's tinny voice called out in Nez Perce, "Woman with Iron Fist, Black Frog, Buffalo Woman, come."

An instant later three faces stared in silent dismay as Ford broke the news of Chief Joseph's capture. Birdie's eyes were as sharp as malachite when they met his. "I will tell the people," she retorted, softly.

"Then may we walk for a bit?" Ford's hand closed over hers.

"You have come to say goodbye." She pointed to where Esther and Ja'meena strolled into the darkness with Ansel and Isaiah.

****

Ford regarded Birdie's beauty, his body longing for her nearness. She was such a puzzle to him that sometimes he didn't know what to say or do in her presence. "I'm a soldier. It's my duty to obey orders."

Concern darkened her face. "If Chief Joseph and his people are being sent far away, then what is to happen to us?"

Tenderly his hands went around her shoulders and held her close. "Colonel Culpepper continues to await word from the big chief in Washington. Don't worry. You'll still be here when I return." In the back of his mind he knew he was trying to convince himself as much as he was Birdie.

Unconsciously, she leaned her head against his shoulder. Ford read the play of emotions across her face and for the first time sensed her true vulnerability. He leaned forward, and his fingers closed with an oddly possessive gesture around her arm. Shocked by the total unexpectedness of his action, Birdie turned so that she fully regarded his face. As she did so, the heavy coat she wore gaped open to reveal a thin muslin petticoat. The cold air caused the pert thrust of her bare nipples to press against the white gauzy material.

His thumb grazed a caressing passage between her inner arm and the soft roundness of her breast beneath the undergarment. "Come to bed with me, Birdie," he whispered in a voice filled with passion.

The hot-blooded maleness of him was like a powerful whirlpool that threatened to draw him into its vortex.

Birdie stifled the moan of pleasure that rose to her lips as his fingertips dipped down to stroke the sensitive contour of her thigh. Ford longed to drown himself in oblivious ecstasy and feel the agonizing joy of her surrender.

With slow reluctance she drew back from the sweet abyss, attempting to pry his fingers from her arm. She whispered at last in a strangled voice, "Do not treat me like a Comanche whore."

But instead of releasing her he captured her in his arms. Birdie raised her hands defensively to form a barrier between them. She pushed against his chest, and reared back in angry defiance, her eyes not flinching from his hot gaze. "How much more must I give?" She choked on a sob. "At least leave me with my pride."

Without warning he released his grip on her shoulders, pushing her from him so that she stumbled backward and was left trembling in the cold.

"Goodbye, Captain Thackery." Birdie ran back to the storehouse, slamming the door behind her.

That night Ford climbed into bed and lay trembling between the blankets in his own cold bed. Birdie's words echoed in his ears: *Do not treat me like a whore.*

****

After a long, fitful night, Birdie finally drifted off to sleep sometime before dawn. She understood now that whatever bit of trust she might have formed with Ford had completely evaporated. He obviously was no better than the drunken trappers or warriors before and after a battle who used women to satisfy their own hot-blooded lust. This thought filled her with desolation. Her emotions were held so tight inside her that she felt she was her own prisoner.

The conversations between Maria and Esther about their weddings and the love and respect from their husbands had held Birdie rapt. So different from when a warrior claimed a woman as his property.

She had envisioned this same type of adoration from Ford. She wanted to lie with him, but only as a wife that shares a bed with a husband.

Chapter Sixteen

Ford stood on the porch in front of Colonel Culpepper's office. He cast a glance along the line of cavalrymen standing next to their patient mounts and awaiting orders, the covered wagons filled with supplies, and then toward the storehouse. The Nez Perce and other captives stood stoic, their faces void of emotion. Even the children remained quiet. Birdie, Esther, and Ja'meena huddled together.

In the predawn hours a steady snow sifted down promising a cold, miserable journey. He wasn't sure how he had managed it, but he'd caught a few hours of sleep before that little voice inside his head woke him.

He forced a smile toward Birdie. She faced him, boldness in her gaze. Even from the distance he noticed the nerve that twitched beneath her right eye. His gut somehow knew she felt alone and isolated. How many times had she expressed her uncertainty about her future? And now he was leaving. Dread slammed into the pit of his stomach, threatening to undo him. He prayed the telegram sealing her fate would be further delayed until his return.

He pulled his gloves on and tugged the hat down tighter on his head. Despite an obsessive need to go to Birdie, he stepped off the porch and strode to his horse. Accepting the reins from the trooper, he mounted the chestnut gelding and settled in the saddle. "Give the order, Sergeant Major."

Sergeant Major Miller swung easily into the saddle. He turned slightly to face the line of expectant troopers, and bellowed, "Mount up. Column of two."

Ford lifted his hand and signaled. He called, "Forward!" He gigged the gelding, and they entered the track leading from the fort and toward Bear Paw Mountains.

****

On a Friday, four days after the departure of Ford and his troop, the duty officer rapped on the storehouse door. He opened it and called, "Miss Dix?"

"Yes?" She stepped forward.

He tipped his hat. "I have a message from Mrs. Culpepper, ma'am. She invites you and Misses Bullard and Pickett to join her for tea and cakes. I am instructed to call for you ladies at two o'clock prompt to escort you to her home."

Birdie frowned up at the young man. "Is she afraid we have forgotten the way and will get lost?"

His eyes shone with amusement at her response. "No, ma'am. For reasons of safety, ma'am."

She acknowledged his comment with a nod. "I must shut the door. It is cold."

"But, ma'am, you will be ready?"

"We will."

Her mind ranged back to the incidents since Ford's departure, especially on gelding day when the young stallions were neutered. She had paused to admire a particular broad-chested, well-muscled chestnut stallion. Men tormented the brutish animal until it reared and lunged at them with bared teeth. She recalled how frightened and panicked she had been when someone left the corral gate open and the monstrous horse thundered through it and straight toward her. Towering above her, it had reared and pawed the air, its mouth open and yellow teeth ready to rip a chunk out of her. No man, soldier or spectator, had raced to her rescue. Instead their laughter had risen to a deafening roar. It was the old warrior Spotted Pony who had rushed forward on crippled legs and flapped a blanket in front of the stallion, causing it to veer away. She had beaten a hasty retreat to the storehouse.

Other incidents included someone locking Ja'meena in the outhouse and then setting fire to dried brush so that she nearly stifled to death before anyone heard her distressed screams. None of them dared venture outside for a breath of fresh air for fear of slingshot attacks.

Colonel Culpepper had ordered an investigation, to no avail.

Esther nudged Birdie's arm. "I suppose it's too farfetched to think Nora simply desires the pleasure of our company."

Flames from the lanterns burned steadily but now began to dip and flutter as if being teased by the wind. Birdie's gaze flew to the door and then to the one window in the room, the only sources through which a breeze could flow. Someone had opened the window and tossed a yellow-and-black-striped feral cat through the opening. Hissing and snarling yowls, coupled with agitated shouts and children's screams, set up a ruckus that brought two guards bursting through the storeroom door.

The cat, seeing its escape route, dashed through the opening and disappeared beneath the nearest building.

Birdie swallowed hard against the dryness in her throat. She drew an audible breath of relief. Still, she wasn't sure if it was anger or fright that trembled her voice. "It does no good to complain. Even Nora is helpless to stop this meanness."

Ja'meena glowered. "If I could put a curse on all of them, I would."

Esther laughed in derisive humor. "And I would help you."

At precisely two o'clock, the officer of the day rapped at the door, then opened it. He said, "Ladies, follow me."

Guards huddled near campfires, talking and warming their hands. Birdie felt the stares of the men come full weight on them as she, Esther, and Ja'meena trod through the white slush. The wind howled like an unseen specter around the buildings. Though she gathered the woolen scarf tighter over her head and around her throat, her fingers were chilled and her feet numb with cold. It was a brief trek from the storehouse to Nora Culpepper's parlor when they stumbled through the front door on a heavy gust of wind.

"My gracious, give me your coats and go warm yourselves by the fire." Nora Culpepper gestured toward the fireplace. "The colonel will join us momentarily."

Birdie glanced reflexively toward Esther and Ja'meena.

Sincerity filled Colonel Culpepper's voice. "What I would like more than anything is to express my apologies for the misdeeds committed against you ladies, and the others. There is no excuse for this kind of bias."

Nora directed them to sit. She offered a tray of delicate tea cups rimmed in gold and adorned with lavender flowers. She busied herself pouring tea and offering lemon cookies.

Birdie wrapped her chilled fingers gratefully around the hot cup as she sat back in one of the tufted chairs. She lifted the cup to her lips and blew gently, careful not to slosh the liquid over the rim. She savored the hot fragrant steam that wafted up into her face. With wariness she knew Esther and Ja'meena, like her, waited for the colonel to break the silence.

He stood, his hands clasped behind his back. He cleared his throat. "Ladies, I've heard from the Bureau of Indian Affairs. For several hours I have pondered how to break the news."

Birdie felt the little warning prickle along her spine. She and her sisters said nothing.

He began at last in a low baritone voice. "You already know that Chief Joseph and his people are on their way to Oklahoma Indian Territory, a very long way from Montana. President Hays has ordered that the Nez Perce in my custody will be sent to Colville Reservation in Washington territory. Each person or family will live in a log cabin. There is a school for the children."

"What of us, Colonel? Will we also go to this reservation?" Esther wanted to know.

The glance he exchanged with Nora did not go unnoticed by the women. "Mrs. Culpepper and I have discussed many options for each of you." He went into great detail about the possibilities. "Our best solution, of course, is possibly a convent where you can live out your life in peace, without fear of retribution like you have experienced at the fort. There is a convent in Texas."

Birdie still felt frozen inside. "When must we decide?"

He released a long sigh. "Within the hour. I have already issued orders to have wagons and supplies and a military escort ready to leave by midday tomorrow. Please tell your people."

The tea scalded Birdie's throat as she swallowed it. She retorted, the illusory moment of what he'd shared and what she understood swallowed up in angry sparks. "*Our people*...the Nez Perce say we are *not* of them. Elmira Ledbetter and her friends say we are *not* white. Now you say to tell *my* people." Her lips lifted sardonically. "Who are we, Colonel Culpepper, and where do we belong?"

Tears of anger splashed her eyes at the total unjustness of their situation. Simmering below the surface with anger and other unnamed emotions, she spoke for a long time in Pawnee to Esther.

Esther set her cup aside. She stood up from the chair. "Birdie forgets her English when she is this upset. She has asked me to speak."

Esther gave an uneasy smile and clasped her hands together. "Knowing this day would come, we have talked many times and made our decision a long time ago. Maria Alvarez is from Texas. She spoke often of the nuns and the poor living conditions at the convents. She also spoke of the cruel treatment they enacted on the orphans. We choose not to go to a convent. We have no money, no suitable clothes, and beyond prostituting ourselves in saloons, we have no skills to exist in so-called proper society. No matter how far and wide we travel or to what towns, there will always be people like Elmira Ledbetter who will unjustly judge us."

Her brows gathered and a frown flitted across her face. "Maria Alvarez desires to return to Texas. She has family and is certain they will open their arms to her and her daughter. Eighteen years Birdie has lived among the Pawnee, the Comanche, and the Nez Perce. For me, between the Hunkpapa and the Nez Perce, I was captive for twenty-five years. Our hair color, skin, and eye color set us apart, yet we have become more Indian than white. We choose to go to this reservation you speak of."

Nora gasped and pressed her hands against her cheeks.

Esther remained standing. She did not look at Nora.

Ja'meena stood. She reached out to link arms with Esther. "I have asked to speak for myself. My home in South Carolina was destroyed by the Yankee blue-bellies and then scavenged by the carpetbaggers. Four years ago, I was on my way to California with dear friends who were like family, with dreams of building a new life. The Cheyenne changed that dream when they murdered my only remaining family." She shuddered. "There are days when I can still feel the stinging lashes of willow rods across my back. I am educated and play the piano, and yet as a black woman where is my place in polite society?" She faced her hosts. "The expression on your faces answers that question." She released Esther's arm to grip her hand. "Birdie and Esther are now my family. I go where my sisters go. Perhaps at the Colville Reservation I might secure a position as a teacher—with a letter of recommendation from you, Colonel Culpepper, of course."

He nodded his assent.

Birdie had regained her composure, and when she spoke her voice was soft, her words measured. "Nora, you have been a good friend. I shall never forget you." She turned to the colonel. "Our belongings are meager. You will not have to wait on us tomorrow."

As they said their goodbyes, Nora's eyes glittered with tears. "What about Captain Thackery and Sergeants Miller and Bohanan? I was certain a few budding romances were in the making."

Birdie heaved a sad sigh and deferred to Esther to answer.

"They are all honorable men, but they are old bachelors set in their ways and married to the cavalry. There is no place in their lives for another wife."

Nora stood in the partially opened doorway of her home. She waved goodbye and disappeared inside.

A snapping chill nipped at Birdie's ankles as she and her sisters sprinted across the yard. Inside the storehouse, she lay on a narrow cot, her knees drawn up to her chest as she shivered beneath the quilt. So many things weighed on her mind.

Chapter Seventeen

It took a while for him to get settled. Ford rode with his head down, daydreaming about Birdie. With time, the fort stretched out behind him and the land roughened up, going hilly, with timbered draws slashing down and between the mountain crevices.

The column traveled at a leisurely pace, even though he wanted to nudge his horse along, accomplish his mission, and return posthaste to the fort. Weeks ago, he'd come to the realization that he needed a change in his life. The years of war had hardened him. He wondered if he still had the capacity to live a normal life filled with compassion and humility. Didn't he deserve a rest? He'd be thirty-seven his next birthday. He'd pledged his life to a military career, and he was much too young to consider retirement. What he'd once sworn never to consider, a wife and children, he now longed for with a need he found surprising.

He'd not come to this astonishing realization until Birdie came into his life. She was honest, and sweet, and giving, and she'd been hurt the way no woman should suffer. Her trust in men and people in general was fragile. He rubbed the knot of nerves at the back of his neck. He'd earned a small fraction of her trust, and he'd also put a serious dent in that trust.

"I'll get it back if…"

"What's that you say, Cap'n?" Ansel cut a glance

toward Ford.

He hadn't realized he'd spoken out loud. "It's not important." He gigged his horse into a lope. "Let's pick up the pace, Sergeant Major." The Bear Paw Mountains and General Miles awaited them.

On Friday, their fourth day out, Ford led his men along the trail. His keen eyes probed the ground for tracks of unshod ponies. He did not intend to blunder into an unexpected ambush by hostiles who refused to accept their way of life had ended. His course of action was obvious: to deliver food, medicine, ammunition, and further aid General Miles in the delivery of Chief Joseph and his people to the railhead in Livingston, some two hundred and seventy miles, and that didn't count the distance from Fort Ellis to the foot of the Bear Paw Mountains.

What could be simpler?

The morning sun lulled the land into wakefulness. The plod of horses, the muttered epitaphs of cold, saddle-weary men, and the rustle and crack of brittle underbrush disturbed the silence.

In the evenings, Ford had consulted the roughly drawn map given to him by Colonel Culpepper, courtesy of General Miles, and had discussed plans of action with his subordinates in the event of an attack from renegade bands that had not yet surrendered. He kept his gelding to a steady, unhurried pace so as not to unnecessarily tax any of the cavalry mounts or the wagon horses. He would push his men as far as stamina allowed.

He rode directly in the center of the trail indicated on the map. He was not a man who liked surprises. He preferred control. As the trail threaded through the jagged peaks, he cantered through patches of shimmering mist, and his men followed.

He was distracted from his thoughts when a glimmer of something in the sunlight flashed. Ansel said, "I see it too, Cap'n. Off to the east in that tree line 'bout two hundred yards."

Ford turned in his saddle and commanded, "Front and center, First Sergeant."

Isaiah spurred his mount forward. "Yassuh, I sees it, too."

Ford had just opened his mouth to give instructions when a startled cry interrupted him. He recognized the particular whir of an arrow.

A trooper gasped, an arrow buried in his throat, and he dropped like a rag doll from the saddle and slammed to the ground. His startled gelding plunged ahead, then back-stepped with grace.

Ford leaned from his saddle, hand outstretched, reaching for the reins. The reins flirted with Ford's gloved fingers before being whisked away by the frightened animal. Ford muttered a curse, "Damn bunch of green horses." He'd pick up the gelding later.

His eyes ranged the forest for the attacker's hiding place, anticipating more assaults. "First Sergeant, order the men to fan out. Rifles ready. Hold fire until the enemy is visible." His commands were succinct as he brought his own prancing gelding under control. "Sergeant Major, keep the men moving. I'll see to Trooper Daily."

Isaiah obeyed. He shouted the order to fan out. He rode down the line. "Stay alert. Rifles ready. Hold fire until the cap'n gives the command."

Ford felt the uneasiness spreading through the

ranks as he galloped toward the downed trooper. He wasted no time, leaping from the saddle. The surprised, glazed-over eyes told him all he needed to know. He lifted the young lad's limp body and hefted it over the saddle, then leaped to the horse's rump. Putting the spurs to him, he raced to one of the empty wagons. "Hold up."

The driver hauled up and handed the reins to the man seated next to him. He jumped to the ground to grab the body. "Are we under attack, sir?"

"Not yet. Stay alert, but keep this wagon moving."

In less than five minutes, Ford had traced back to the head of the column. He shouted, "Sergeant Major, take command. First Sergeant—with me. Pick two of your best sharpshooters. We're going hunting."

Riding tight to avoid being an easy target, Ford and his hunters pushed their horses into an easy lope up a gentle slope and through lush belly-high grass. He lifted his hand and signaled to halt. He knew what was going on in Isaiah's troubled eyes. Each battle, big or small, might be a soldier's last. Ford reined his horse around to look at his men. "You all know what we're up against. With rifles, and a little luck, whoever is up there could pick off any one of us before we even see them."

There was grimness in each man's eyes. One of the sharpshooters forced a smile. "We knew the odds when we took on the assignment, Captain."

Ford nodded. He remained in the lead. His was by far in the most dangerous position. He accepted it without question. This was his job. He slipped his saddle gun from the scabbard, and touched heels to his horse's ribs.

Like ghosts, ten renegade Sioux, their faces painted the garish red and black of their clan, emerged from the dense mist that covered the forested side of the mountain. As they swept toward Ford and his hunting party, rifles blazing, yodeling war cries reverberated through the mists. It was enough to give a man the willies. Ford's gelding moved of its own volition toward the enemy. Tensed, Ford levered a cartridge into his Winchester. He shouted to his companions, "Fire at will."

A rifle cracked. Then another. A Sioux warrior cradled his wounded shoulder. Another warrior screamed as he drove his heels into a sturdy mustang's sides, plowing toward Ford. The animal reared and neighed in terror as it plunged against Ford's chestnut gelding. Ford managed to kick free of the stirrups to roll away from the slashing hooves and crushing weight.

The warrior had unsheathed a knife and now crouched low, circling Ford. He knew that no one needed to tell this savage how to kill. Given the opportunity, he would eviscerate Ford and then brag about his victory. Ford whipped his sidearm from its holster and without hesitation fired just as the massive frame slammed into him. Eyes filled with hatred glared at Ford. It was as if the bullet hadn't fazed him.

"I am Crow Dog. I will cut out your heart and eat it, Blue Coat," he screamed. The Sioux warrior stood like a giant bear of a man, gripping his knife like a terrible steel claw poised for the kill.

The revolver bucked in Ford's fist, and spat flame. Determined, the warrior continued forward as if defying death. Ford steadied his aim, squeezed the trigger, and fired again. He watched as the bullet's impact propelled the man backward on his haunches, leaving a fountain of crimson to spout from his chest.

The fight was over as quickly as it had begun. Ford gingerly cradled his arm. Sticky red wetness stained the fingertips of his glove. There had been the violent clamor of guns. Now came the equally unsettling aftermath of stillness.

Isaiah, leading two horses, walked toward Ford. Despite the coldness pervading the morning, sweat glistened on the sergeant's brow. He sleeved an arm across his eyes. "I reckon we whupped 'em, Cap'n."

Ford heaved a sigh. "Any casualties?"

"Nah-suh. Well, 'ceptin' Trooper Daily, God rest his soul. He was a good boy." His expression grew grim. "Reckon you'd best let me tend yo' arm right away, suh."

Ford chuckled. "Just a scratch, First Sergeant." He accepted the reins, glad that his trusty horse was none the worse for wear. Weary and his arm throbbing, he climbed into the saddle. He leaned forward to glide a hand down the long chestnut neck. "Once again you've earned your oats, ol' son."

Despite himself, Ford trembled. His breath clouded the air, and he wondered if the sun would break through to drive the chill away. Two bald eagles dipped and soared and floated on the breeze and seemed to be a moving evocation. What was it that Birdie had said about the eagles they'd watched not so long ago? An omen.

"What'll we do with 'em, suh?"

Ford frowned down at the sprawled bodies. Nodding toward the two sharpshooters, he said, "These men were once great warriors. It's tough giving up generations of freedom. The least we can do is show them respect. Since we don't have time to build scaffoldings on which to place their bodies, turn them face down and their feet toward the south."

He worked to keep the pain from his voice as he tightened the hat against his head. "Let's get back to the column. We have three more days of travel before reaching General Miles."

"Yo' heard the cap'n. Get them bodies turned over. Then mount up and don't let no grass grow under yo' hosses' feet."

Ford smiled inwardly. He knew without doubt that once they were bivouacked for the night, Isaiah would hover over him with a bottle of turpentine to tend his wound.

They angled eastward for a while. Ford wanted to put some distance between them and where the attack took place. The going wasn't bad because the land was mostly gentle and flat, rising and falling a little.

He gradually eased the travel toward the north. He kept the troopers going at a good clip, trotting the horses for a while and then loping them some, trying to make as much time as possible. Riding up and down the line, he saw the speed was beginning to tell on the horses. He could feel his chestnut laboring to hold the pace.

"We've made good time, Sergeant Major. Before we lose the light and make camp, keep an eye out for the dry fork of Beaver Creek. I don't want to take a chance on missing it in the dark. According to the map, there's fresh water and a straight track to General Miles."

Ansel acknowledged with a nod.

Eventually they found the fork and the creek. Ansel gave the order to dismount and set up camp.

Ford unsaddled his own horse, allowing a trooper to lead the gelding to the remuda. By the time Isaiah approached with a medicine kit, Ford had washed his face and hands in a tin basin provided by the assistant cook. Drying his face, he grimaced. "I'd rather have a cup of coffee laced with brandy than have you hover over me like a mother hen with your home cures."

Isaiah chuckled. "Which would yo' rather have, suh, me motherin' you and gettin' rid of infection or havin' a sawbones whack off yo' arm? Don't reckon yo' could soldier with one arm."

Ford grunted and sat in a chair. He removed his coat and rolled up the sleeve of his uniform blouse. He bit back a curse when Isaiah poured a healthy amount of turpentine into the already festering gash and proceeded to wrap a bandage around his arm. He couldn't remember a time when the old soldier hadn't taken care of him.

Ansel arrived with a plate of scrambled eggs, bacon, hardtack, and a mug of steaming coffee. "Figured you could use some nourishment." He turned to leave. "I've posted the watch, sir."

"You and Isaiah go fill your plates. Come back and join me."

Ford balanced the tin plate on his lap while he took cautious sips of the hot brew. He grinned. Leave it to the sergeant major to add a little medicinal whiskey to the coffee. He reflected on how long Ansel and Isaiah had been with him. These brave and loyal men had become more than soldiers under his command—they were more than friends—almost like family.

He gazed out at the snowcapped mountains. He had a sudden and unusual longing for his boyhood home.

****

Old death has a distinct putrid odor. The hum of blowflies offered a macabre chorus to the boneyard.

"Sweet mother, Cap'n." Ansel lifted the yellow kerchief around his neck to cover his nose. "I think I'm gonna puke up my innards."

Three days had passed since the surprise Indian attack. Ford and his troop had followed a rough trail. Now, he noted the rotting horse carcasses, the remnants of burned wagons, numerous fresh mounds topped with large stones and crosses to mark the graves of brave soldiers, broken lances littering the ground, and mounds both large and small adorned with grass to indicate the Nez Perce burial places. The sight of small graves touched Ford's heart. No woman or child should die under such cruel circumstances.

Here, so far from civilization, the loss of wagons and supplies meant the same eventual outcome: death.

He rode onward and looked. Although he'd been raised in the church, he wasn't a religious man. *Ashes to ashes…dust to dust.* In years to come, with rain and snow and probing winds, the charred remains of the skeletons would be reduced to ashes and returned to the earth.

Ford and his troopers followed the bone-strewn trail for five miles, straight into General Miles' bivouac area.

Sergeant Major Ansel Miller shivered, though the morning sun was warm. "This place makes my skin crawl. How long before we move out, Cap'n?"

"That's up to General Miles, Sergeant Major." Ford lifted his hand to halt the column.

A lean man with steel gray hair and a slight hunch emerged from a tent, his arm in a sling. "Captain Thackery, I presume."

"Take the command, Sergeant Major. Join me in the general's quarters as soon as possible for further orders."

"Right away, Cap'n."

Ford saluted the general. "Yes, sir. It appears you've had a rough go of it." His eyes trailed around the bivouac area until he settled on the Nez Perce captives some distance from the main camp, armed guards posted to detain possible escapees. He harrumphed inwardly. From the ragtag looks of these people, they were too tired and too defeated to make the long trek to the railhead in Livingston and then onward to the hellhole of Indian Territory in Oklahoma.

Chapter Eighteen

A mantle of white draped all of Fort Ellis. Two covered wagons and a supply wagon—their home for the next hundreds of miles—waited in the middle of the yard.

There was no fanfare, no one lined the boardwalks to wave and wish them Godspeed as the band of captives braved the frigid wind to stand next to the wagons.

Spotted Pony, using his new crutches, plodded across the compound, his wife Butterfly Woman at his side. Birdie, Esther, and Ja'meena followed.

The chilling gusts that accompanied the glowering sky buffeted young and old, male and female, puckishly snatching at coats and blankets draped around frail shoulders. Cheeks and noses were brightened to a reddish hue as the small group waited with resignation.

Spotted Pony kicked a clump of muddy snow and pursed his wrinkled lips as he stood in front of Colonel Culpepper and spoke. Esther translated. "If you listen closely, there are words in the wind. The wind is our mother. She says the day of the mighty warrior is no more. We are like old women who no longer have strength to fight. One by one we have been destroyed, too old and too hungry to carry on, our lands stolen. We are driven to the reservations…no longer free to hunt the elk and the buffalo. We have given our sons, our daughters, brothers, and wives. Saaaa…the white man does all this for the yellow metal deep beneath our earth. What more can we give?"

The colonel's face contorted as if a wave of pain had washed over him. "If it were within my power…orders from our big chief in Washington… nasty time of the year to travel." He hunched his shoulders. "I'm at a loss for words."

A deep and painful sigh escaped from Nora Culpepper. She hugged each lady. "Won't you change your minds and stay? I'm certain that with time the colonel can arrange something suitable for you."

Birdie pulled from her grasp. "It is true that we travel to an uncertain future." She offered a tenuous smile. "These are our people now. We cannot leave them. We can only pray that our tomorrows are far better than our yesterdays."

Tilting her chin in defiance as she spotted her nemesis standing in front of the sutler's store, Birdie didn't hide the disgust in her voice. "Elmira Ledbetter has braved the cold to make sure we do not stay behind."

In a rare moment of loathing, Nora spouted, "Damn that woman."

Maria Alvarez stepped forward, clutching her daughter's hand. She blinked back the tears. She spoke in Pawnee. "My heart is filled with words that I cannot speak. You are far braver than I to travel to another unknown future."

Esther hugged the woman and the little girl. "Only the brave and the strong survive what you…what we have endured. Our hearts are gladdened that your sister and brother are coming to take you home." She stepped back.

Ja'meena wrapped her arms around Maria. A sob escaped her lips. "Remember us in your nightly prayers."

Maria nodded.

Birdie clasped Maria's hands. Sometimes silence is more powerful than spoken words.

"Ma'am…" His voice was soft but strong. "I'm Lieutenant Emerson Garrett. You already know Corporal Tibbets. We're your escorts. Will you instruct the people to load themselves in the two front wagons?"

Colonel Culpepper stepped forward. "Lieutenant Garrett, I hold you and your men personally responsible for the safe delivery of *all* these people to the train depot in Livingston. The moment you put them aboard, wire the Indian Agent Ben Haverson at Colville Reservation to meet the train in approximately seven days…eight days at the most. You are to personally travel with them to assure these people are molested in no way." He cut his eyes toward where Birdie, Esther, and Ja'meena waited. "Put your lives on the line if necessary. Understood?"

"Yessir," was spoken in unison.

"Corporal Tibbets…Privates Reece and Smith, after the passengers are secured, you are to return to Fort Ellis. No personal leave time. Understood?" He cast an authoritative glare.

"Lieutenant, wait up. Send a man to fetch Miss Dix's horse," Colonel Culpepper ordered.

She reached out and touched his arm. "I cannot take Gunpowder with me. Spotted Pony says that Indians are not permitted to own horses on the reservation."

Loretta C. Rogers

"But you are not—"

Birdie cut off his response. "I am what so-called respectable people have said of me. Besides, I could not bear it if he was mistreated by a new owner. I am returning him to Captain Thackery."

"I understand. So be it, then." He cleared the rasp from his throat. "Belay the order, Lieutenant. The horse stays here."

As if she had forgotten, Nora held forth a sealed cardboard box. "Ja'meena, inside are slates, boxes of chalk, several primers, and a few classics. I do hope you enjoy *Wuthering Heights, Jane Eyre*, and *A Tale of Two Cities*." She sighed. "And my personal favorite, a book of sonnets by Shakespeare."

Tears welled in Ja'meena's eyes as she accepted the box and clutched it to her chest. "Nora, this is the most precious gift I've ever received. I promise to use all the books wisely, especially the primers to help teach the children how to read."

Nora said solemnly, "There is a journal for you, Esther and Birdie, nib pens and ink pots. You must write down your stories. For personal healing if need be, but also because the three of you have made history that must one day be shared with the world."

Her brows gathered in a dark gloom, Ja'meena allowed a Spartan smile to curve her lips.

"Miss Dix, ladies—" Impatience tinged the lieutenant's voice. "Ten to a wagon."

Birdie simply nodded. She was in no hurry to begin another arduous journey. Still, in the language of the Nez Perce, she instructed each person, dividing the two mothers with children, herself, Esther, Ja'meena, and the youngest of the remaining women to the first wagon, and Spotted Pony with Butterfly Woman, the aged warriors, and older women in the second wagon.

After seeing everyone loaded, she swallowed back the quaver in her voice. "You have been a true friend, Nora. May Mother Earth and the Great Spirit Father smile upon you always." She squinted toward Elmira Ledbetter. *And may Kaga bedevil you for the rest of your miserable life.*

She reached for Nora's hand, giving it one last squeeze before she hurried to her home on wheels.

She clenched the fullness of her skirt with slender hands, lifted her foot to the step, and with a little hop was on the tailgate. She sucked in a deep breath to halt the sadness welling up within her, and blinking unwanted tears, glanced about, her eyes settling on the closed door of Ford's cabin. After all, Indian women were not allowed to cry.

Her heart tripped over itself. To redirect her thoughts to something less emotional, she parted the canvas curtain and entered the wagon's cozy confines. Much to her surprise, bunk beds lined both walls, and a new quilt lay neatly folded at the end of each bed. A lantern swung from the rib of an iron center beam. Squeezed beneath the bottom bunks were two trunks. Nora had thought of everything.

Emotionally drained, it was not at all surprising to her that the room seemed to tilt unnaturally, leaving her swaying on her feet and blinking against an encroaching dizziness. In desperation, she clutched the nearest bedpost for support and rested her brow against the cool wood until gradually the feeling subsided. She had eaten very little since Ford's departure. What sleep she had finally managed wasn't worth noting. No matter the hardships one had to face, life had to go on.

Yet it was so terribly hard. Birdie groaned inwardly. All she knew was that she felt something deeply for Ford, an emotion that had frightened her. A stirring that she'd never before experienced. She was tormented by his kiss. She had pushed him away, had run from him like a frightened deer facing a mountain lion, and now she would never see him again. Emotions she didn't understand tugged at her.

"Birdie, are you okay?" She hadn't realized that Esther and Ja'meena had pulled a wooden chest to the wagon's center and seated her on it. "You are as pale as a winter moon." It was Esther's voice that broke through the gloom.

Sighing wearily, she looked up. "I guess I forgot to eat."

The wagon lurched forward, eliciting nervous squeals from the children.

To lighten the mood and to dismiss their concerns, Birdie looked about. "Which bed is mine?"

Ja'meena said, "The two bottom bunks are for the children. Esther and I have claimed the middle bed." She chortled. "You are younger and spryer. We left a top bunk for you."

Pushing herself from the trunk, she used the bottom and second beds as a ladder. Looking down from the top, she said, "I will rest until the wagon stops."

She unfolded the multicolored quilt and cocooned it around her body. She closed her eyes and listened to snowflakes on canvas, the rhythmic patter hypnotic. Her last thought as her eyelids closed was that she had brought about the turmoil herself and now she didn't know how to cope with it. Ford Thackery was no better than any other man she had encountered. He wanted her body but not her. A quiver swept through her and surged straight to her woman parts as she recalled the soft touch of his lips against hers, how his hands had dropped to her waist and had caressed her slender curves.

Perhaps the many weeks' travel from Montana to Washington territory might resolve her inner confusion and conflicts.

Chapter Nineteen

A freezing temperature and a snowy mist shrouded the darkness. The lantern cast a shadowy eeriness inside the covered wagon. The women and children huddled under their blankets. All were thankful for the light's stingy heat.

Five days of travel seemed like an eternity. Lieutenant Garrett had informed them that they should arrive at the depot in two days. Fully clothed and wearing woolen socks, Birdie propped against the bedposts, the quilt pulled to her chin. "Ja'meena, is this train that awaits us like the covered wagon trains that come to the fort?"

Ja'meena raised on an elbow. Her dark face crinkled into thoughtfulness. "I have heard some call it an Iron Horse, but it is not a horse and doesn't resemble one. Hmm, let me think how best to describe it."

After a pensive moment, she said, "A train is like a very long black snake separated by joints like the glass-tailed lizard—when one section breaks off another can replace it. It is on iron wheels and rolls on a long track made of metal instead of dirt. The head of the snake is called a locomotive, and to keep it running, two men called engineers feed wood into its belly. Does this make sense?"

"Oh, yes. Can a horse outrun a train?"

"I believe a horse can outdistance a train for only a

short time. A horse gets tired and after a while runs out of speed. A train never gets tired, and it only slows down when it is hungry for more wood."

"Esther, did you ever see a train or ride on one?" Ja'meena wanted to know.

Esther offered an easy smile. "Though it has been many years, yes, I do remember seeing a train. I used to daydream about escaping Mr. Bullard and all the places I would travel. I never had enough money for a ticket." She was thoughtful for a moment. "After I was captured, there were times when I did not care what happened to me. I took the moving about, the running from the enemy, in stride. Trains and dreams and civilization ceased to exist."

A long silence followed. Birdie seemed to know what Esther was thinking. "Once again our future is uncertain." She was thoughtfully quiet for a while. "Ja'meena, you will continue teaching me to read and write?"

"Of course. Why wouldn't I?"

Birdie touched her heart. "In here, I sense a change is coming, to all of us. I don't know what or when. It isn't good or bad, just different...I think."

"Baaah!" The women jumped at the fierceness of Spotted Pony's voice as his gnarled hands pulled back the canvas and his wrinkled face peered through the slit.

"Why are you lurking about in the dark, old one? You should be in bed warming your woman's feet," Esther scolded.

"One cannot ignore when nature calls. I am old and I have to pee more often than when I was young." Spotted Pony stared at them. "You women are fortunate. You whine like frightened rabbits. I was once a mighty warrior and have many injuries from combat. What scars do you bear?" He leered at them. "You women are lucky your scars are few."

Birdie jumped from the top bunk to face him. The chill that moments ago had her shivering had now turned to scorching heat. "Oh, some of us have many. But we carry them in our souls, where they cannot be seen." She made a shooing motion with her hand. "Be gone, old man. Go look deep into Butterfly Woman's eyes. Perhaps you will see the depth of her wounds, and when you do, be ashamed for never acknowledging her strength to carry them in silence."

Like a shadow he faded into the darkness.

Esther put an arm around Birdie. "If it were possible, I would turn back time and take away the sorrow we have had to live with these many years."

As they settled down for the night, Birdie forced herself to sleep until she could no longer bear the fullness in her bladder. Groaning, she slid quietly from the bunk. She groped in the darkness for her boots and slipped her feet inside. Carefully, so as not to awaken the others, she parted the canvas and lifted her legs over the tailgate and eased to the snowy ground.

Squinting in the blackness, she sprinted a short distance from the wagons until she found a clump of bushes, then hiked up her skirts and squatted to relieve herself. Finished, she stood and quickly rearranged her clothing, wishing she had thought to bring the quilt for warmth.

"Woman with Iron Fist." Her name barely a whisper, she turned, annoyed that one of the soldiers might have followed her.

Momentarily startled into silence, she said, "You!"

Her heart thudded against her chest like a slow pounding, impending doom.

Fear surging, Birdie took a running step. His hand grabbed her shoulder and wrenched her around to face him. His teeth showed a savage snarl as he drew back his fist. The blow, fast and furious, slammed against her jaw. "Bitch! You won't escape me again."

Her last thought before she lost consciousness was the crazed lust she saw in Levi High Eagle's eyes.

****

Grabbed and gagged, and quickly bound, Birdie knew her struggles were futile. High Eagle had thrown her over his shoulder. White hot terror stabbed at her as he ran through the darkness.

"Hey, what the—"

A startled voice rang out in front of them. Instantly there came a sickening squish of suction as a blade jabbed and withdrew from the soldier who had happened upon them. He collapsed to the ground.

His grunt had not been loud enough to alert the others, but he was able to fire his rifle to sound an alarm.

Jostled and bounced, Birdie continued to try and scream against the foul-smelling rag bound around her mouth. She was lowered to the ground for only a moment before being hoisted into the saddle to sit in front of High Eagle. Repulsed by his rancid smell, she hunched forward, not wanting to lean against him.

He laughed. "So you do not want to touch me? That's too bad. You are High Eagle's woman now. Go ahead and scream."

Birdie coughed. Her words sounded muffled against the gag. She repeated, "I can't breathe."

159

As if understanding, he warned as he pushed the cloth from her mouth, "Scream and you will die."

Slowly her mind cleared. She wiped the back of a trembling hand across a bloodied lip. Birdie remembered something another captive woman had told her many years ago. *Be strong. Never show fear, no matter how badly your legs are shaking.*

Drinking in gulps of air, she said, "You won't get away with this. The soldiers will come after you. They will find you."

He wrapped his arms around her. "Not likely. I am a damned good Pawnee scout." One hand squeezed her breasts and he said huskily, "You make me want to hurry to where I am taking you so I can look at you, and then I have a big prize for you. Big like a stallion."

A multitude of disparaging names tempted her tongue, but she held still, aware she trod on dangerous ground. Her sharp fingernails bit into the bony top of his hand. He balled his fist and bashed the side of her head. It took every ounce of her willpower to remain conscious.

Swallowing against hysteria, she told herself that all she could do was wait for an opportunity to get away from him. Hope soared inside her when she heard the lieutenant's voice.

Lieutenant Garrett shouted, "Corporal Tibbets, who fired that shot?"

"Wasn't me, sir," Tibbets responded.

"Dammit, man, find out."

"Lieutenant…Lieutenant Garrett, Birdie isn't in her bunk," Esther screamed as she climbed down from the wagon.

"Where the hell is she?" he growled.

At the sound of her name, Birdie drew a breath to scream. High Eagle wrapped his hand over her mouth, painfully pinching her cheeks together until her jawbones ached. He spurred the horse, setting him into a full gallop.

From far off she could hear Esther and Ja'meena calling her name.

As they raced through the darkness, Birdie knew she was in terrible danger. The Pawnee were notorious for their atrocities against captive women. Added to that was the fact that High Eagle's attempt to molest her had led to his imprisonment at Fort Ellis.

But even as the horror of what awaited her coursed through her mind, she struggled to keep a clear head, ready to seize the first opportunity to escape.

They rode into a creek. Icy water splashed against their legs and up to their thighs. The horse stumbled, causing High Eagle to wrap his arm tighter around Birdie's waist. She was certain the thing gouging into her back was the hilt of High Eagle's hunting knife. It was tucked into his waistband. All she had to do was twist around, jerk backward, and snatch the knife from its sheath before plunging it into his villainous heart. She would have one chance and only one chance. If she failed, he would kill her.

She played the scene over and over in her mind. No matter how many times she envisioned it, the outcome was the same—him falling off the horse and pulling her down with him. She would either drown or freeze to death. There was nothing to do but wait until High Eagle either stopped for the night to rest or they arrived at wherever he was taking her.

The night wore on, and Birdie wondered if he ever

planned to stop and rest. At last she felt the horse slowing just a bit and dared to hope they had reached their destination. She squinted into the inky night only to see dark shadows hovering on both sides. Perhaps they were in a deep ravine. With the striking of iron horseshoes against rock and the slow way the horse was walking, she surmised they were traveling over stony ground. Her fuzzy brain tried to comprehend where she was.

Distress and the horse's slow, rocking pace added to her fatigue. She willed herself to stay awake and alert, but before long, her eyes closed and her head lolled against High Eagle's chest.

Chapter Twenty

High Eagle smiled. It was good that she slept. He would stop soon for he also was tired. She was his. He would make her his slave. It was the Pawnee way. She would do his bidding and he would teach her a thousand ways to pleasure him.

In the mountains were many caverns with overhangs to hide the entrances. He guided his horse into one such cave and continued deep inside and away from the opening. He slid from the saddle. Hoisting Birdie over his shoulder, he carried her to the makeshift bed he had created.

As he laid his prize on the bed, he paused to unbutton her coat. He spread it wide and slid his hands inside, savoring the warmth as he caressed the mounds of her breasts in a heated anticipation. "Soon...soon," he promised, "I will have you again and again."

Her eyes fluttered open. She blinked to bring her surroundings into focus. The throbbing in her head brought a soft groan. Her muscles tensed as his fingers sought the buttons on her blouse. She did not try to conceal her repugnance. "Touch me and I will find a way to cut off that *thing* you are so proud of and stuff it down your throat."

He laughed at her bravado and grabbed at the bulge that had built between his legs. "I will gladly show you my *thing*. Many women have cried at the sight of it."

She knew taunting him was a bad idea. Maybe if she goaded him enough he would become careless and she could grab his knife. "You mean the women cried in disappointment because your *wasatch* is the size of a small boy's." She continued pushing. "You know what the wise grandmothers say—'He who boasts the loudest hides the truth.' " She laughed. "The truth is the only women you have ever satisfied are the ones in your imagination."

A heavy sigh gave evidence of his displeasure. He shook his head slowly, as if sorrowed by her statement. "I am not as lenient as I used to be. It will be your fault if I hurt you."

Birdie spat, "When were the *dog-eaters* ever lenient? You are nothing more than a low-bellied snake that needs to slither back into your slimy hole."

"Snake, is it?" He snarled at the insults. "*Dog-eater*? I'll show you." He gathered the lapels of her coat in a fist and snatched her forward. He backhanded her again and again, venting his desire for vengeance.

Birdie struggled to remain alert beneath the harsh battering. The coppery taste of blood filled her mouth. She clenched her jaws against the painful blows. "Coward. Is that why your people call you by your real name—*Mud Pony*?"

She sought to swallow the hard lump that had welled up in her throat. She lifted her chin obstinately. Her sharp tone sliced through the cave. "You won't get away with this. My name is on the paper with Spotted Pony and Butterfly Woman, and Buffalo Woman and Ugly Frog, saying that we are to ride on the great iron horse to Washington. I will be missed. The Army will search for me. Captain Thackery will hunt you down and take your scalp. Let me go. I will not reveal your name or your hideout."

High Eagle gazed down at her with sardonic amusement. His scornful smile mocked her until she balled her fist and let it fly, catching him smartly on the chin. The force reeled him backward on his heels.

With a strength borne of desperation, she swept around him as she fled. An enraged snarl emitted from his lips and increased in volume as he grabbed her arm and swung her around to slam her hard against his chest. With the strength of a steel trap, he pinned her arms against her side. He lowered his mouth to hers. She tossed her head from side to side.

"You are the scum of the earth. I do not give you breeding rights." She managed to hawk a wad. The spittle slid down his chin to land on a button of his blue Army jacket.

"I've had enough from you, bitch." He pulled back a fist, intending to let it fly. "I'll beat you to a bloody pulp." Rage mottled his face. His jaw tightened.

She knew she would not be able to withstand a beating without slipping into an uncaring oblivion. Concentrating hard, she slid her hand downward to the sash around his waist, allowing her fingers to slip between the folds of the dingy fabric. Gripping the heavy knife in her fist, she snatched it upward, and with all the force she could muster, jabbed the blade into the arm that held her prisoner. As if she were gutting the belly of a buffalo, she ripped the knife downward, tearing through tendon and muscle.

High Eagle yowled with pain. He stumbled backward, holding his arm as he gawked at the bloodied blade clasped in Birdie's hand, then gaped in horror at the widening stream of red darkening his shirt.

Birdie anticipated the need for swift flight and was already catching up her skirts to whirl away. She commanded her feet to run. She heard the stumbling advance of her enemy behind her and knew that if not for his pain, he would overtake her. Her feet flew as she ran half-stumbling toward the cave opening. Her heart kept pace. She prayed he had not unsaddled the horse. Not that it mattered; she could ride bareback as well as any warrior.

His threats echoed off the cave walls, and they encouraged her to keep running, for she well imagined what would happen if he caught her.

She flitted around the corner and knew a moment's relief to see the brown-and-white pinto standing slack-hipped, its head down, and still saddled. She was safe. Barely. She spoke to the animal while gathering the reins. Setting a foot in the stirrup and panting for breath, she wrapped her hands around the saddle horn and was about to swing into the seat.

Panic welled inside her when a hand with the strength of a bear trap wrapped around her ankle. She cried out in alarm and kicked furiously with her free leg, her foot landing a lucky blow against High Eagle's wounded arm.

Clutching the bloodied limb, he stumbled backward, giving her enough momentum to swing into the saddle. Without compunction she snatched the pinto's head around. Gouging her heels deep into its sides, she made the startled horse lunge forward.

"I'll catch you, bitch…you won't be pretty no more when I finish cutting on you! Hear me…bitch! You will beg to die before I am finished with you." She listened to his staggering footfalls as he chased after her. Risking a glance over her shoulder, she watched him sink to his knees, then fall forward.

She guided the horse toward a dim light. Outside the cave, the moon was a thumbnail in a pinking sky. Little warmth from yesterday's sun remained in the high-sided arroyo. Birdie studied her surroundings and tried to figure out where she was. Not wanting to waste time, she pushed the horse forward, hoping that during the time of her unconsciousness High Eagle had picked a direct path to his hideout.

She knew there were labyrinths of ravines, some leading to boxed canyons, and had heard many stories of people getting lost in these mazes never to be seen again. The old ones believed these areas were haunted and steered clear of them. This brought a discouraging thought that, if anyone were to come searching for her, her bones might be bleached white before she was ever found.

Shaking away the dismal thoughts and refocusing, she knew the blow to her jaw from last night had knocked her out for perhaps an hour or more. Then before falling into an exhausted oblivion, they had crossed an icy stream that had deepened up to their thighs. Several times she had roused and glanced upward to see the North Star. It was perhaps another hour or so before riding into the cave and to High Eagle's camp, or had more than a day passed? She would worry about time later.

Her stomach tightened and rumbled. It had been many hours since sharing a pot of stew and fried bread with Esther and Ja'meena. She was weak and weary but plodded onward, hoping High Eagle would bleed to death from his wound, yet fearing he would somehow gather the strength to survive and come after her. And God help her if he did.

She had to find Lieutenant Garrett and the wagons as quickly as possible. She didn't know the way to the train depot, and she didn't have enough strength to travel the long distance back to Fort Ellis.

Her hair hung limp. The cold permeated through her plaid tweed coat, leaving her teeth-chatteringly miserable. Her feet were like blocks of ice inside the damp woolen socks in her boots.

Many times she had endured days of hunger when food was withheld as a form of punishment. She tried not to focus on the gnawing cramps in her stomach. Nonetheless, she grew weaker as morning slipped into midday.

At one point she felt herself slipping from the saddle but at the last minute wrapped her hands around the saddle horn and hauled herself back into the seat. To get her mind off her growing hunger and thirst and the seriousness of her situation, she turned her thoughts to Captain Ford Thackery.

She reached inside her coat and down the neck of her dress to finger the tiny gold bird that dangled from its chain. She remembered staring into eyes so blue they were almost black. It was at that moment she realized Ford was a man with steel in his eyes, and that he would never back down from trouble. She chastised herself for not getting to know him, really getting to know him, before he left the fort. She had strong feelings for him. Could it be called love? With all the cruelty she had been subjected to, was she even capable of love?

She had loved her son but had hated the man who had forcibly planted his seed in her. Had she loved her white mother and father and little brother? She unconsciously shrugged. She'd been so young she didn't remember. She had no answers.

She wanted to relive the magic she had felt in Ford's arms a few short weeks ago. The thought of him, his broad shoulders, muscled arms, and the sensual heat in his blue eyes caused pinpricks of heat to settle between her legs in a slow, deep throb.

She drifted to thinking how safe she had felt in that short moment he'd held her in his arms, and the sweetness of his kiss. She ran her tongue over parched lips trying to recall the pleasant pressure of his lips against hers.

Her eyes swimming with tears, she reminded herself that the only time Indian women were allowed to cry was at the loss of a loved one. She laughed out loud at this thought. The Indians said she was white and the whites said she was Indian. Like not knowing what love was, she didn't know who she was or where she belonged.

She drifted into meandering thoughts while the pinto gelding continued its plodding pace. It was the swishing of his tail that broke into her reverie, and she realized the horse was no longer moving. She stared at the jagged granite peaks that rose like giants blocking her escape.

She felt a distant thud. Lying there looking up at the sky, she barely remembered falling from the saddle. Thankfully, she still gripped the reins in one hand. A mishmash of emotions welled up inside her. She refused to allow the tears to flow. No! She closed her mind to the thoughts bombarding her. She wouldn't allow them to return.

She couldn't help laughing—a strange sound echoing off the walls of the canyon.

Forcing herself to stand, she struggled to lift her foot to the stirrup and to pull herself into the saddle. Weak and racked by hunger, and nearly frozen to the bone, God help her, she was completely lost. She turned the pony around and headed back the way she had come. She hoped.

Her head began to loll. It was getting harder and harder to stay in the saddle. The horse moved slowly, at times lifting its head and snorting. Mountain lions lived in the many caves in these rocky prisons. She had no desire to fall prey to more dangerous creatures—animal or human.

She looked up at the sky. "Mother Earth, Father Sky, hear my cry. I am lost. Show the horse the way."

Her eyes closed… She forced them open. But then she felt herself slumping forward—the saddle horn bruised her chest. Her arms hung limp on either side of the pinto's neck. She inhaled his horse scent…and then darkness enveloped her.

Chapter Twenty-One

Esther and Ja'meena repeatedly called Birdie's name. Esther asked, somewhat perplexed, "Why doesn't she answer?"

Corporal Tibbets yelled, "Lieutenant Garrett, over here. It's Private Reece. He's been knifed in the chest."

The two women trotted after the lieutenant. Garrett knelt on one knee. "Is he alive?"

"I think so, sir. Not for certain."

Esther squatted. "I know a little doctoring." Without hesitation and using nimble fingers, she unbuttoned the supine man's heavy coat and then his blue uniform blouse. She leaned her cheek close to his mouth.

"Well?" the lieutenant demanded.

She stared hard at Garrett and answered in bold defiance. "It is not his day to die. The big metal button on his coat kept the knife from piercing his heart. He bleeds much. The wound must be burnt to stop the bleeding."

"Do what you can for him, ma'am, until we get to Livingston and a doctor." In a low deep voice laced with agitation, he added, "Private Smith, start hitching up the horses. Tibbetts, help me get Reece to his bed in the supply wagon. I want to roll out on the half-hour. Understood?"

Esther pulled back, allowing the wounded soldier

to be lifted from the ground. "Lieutenant, I will require the powder from one of your bullets and a fire stick that you call a match." She placed her hands on her hips and frowned. "If you wish your man to live, you will not move the wagon until I have seared the wound, unless you prefer that I catch his hair on fire instead."

Garrett grumbled, "Very well, then. He is my responsibility. I will assist you."

Nodding, Esther exchanged glances with Ja'meena. In a soft voice, she said, "Send Spotted Pony to collect several pieces of aspen bark. Have Butterfly Woman boil part of them into a tea, and the other pieces are to use as a poultice." She hesitated. "And keep looking for Birdie. I fear that whoever stabbed the private kidnapped Birdie."

Determination rose in Ja'meena's eyes. She hastened to carry out Esther's requests.

An hour later, the lieutenant flashed an appreciative glance at Esther. "That was fine work, Mrs. Bullard. I have learned a valuable lesson in medicine. I didn't know aspen bark was a medicinal tea, or that it could be used as an antibiotic for an open wound." She felt a comforting hand on her shoulder. "How did you learn to cauterize injuries by pouring gunpowder in the wound and lighting it with a match?"

Esther allowed a small grim smile to lighten her features for a moment. "I have learned much in my many years with the Hunkpapa. Medicine and survival are just a few."

Finally, after staring hard at Esther for endless seconds, he rose to his feet, and said, "You will stay and tend to him until we arrive in Livingston."

Her voice was indignant. "Are you asking,

Lieutenant, or is that an order?"

His mouth twitched. "Asking, ma'am."

"Thank you, Lieutenant Garrett."

Fifteen minutes later, Ja'meena rushed to stand on the supply wagon's tailgate. She held out her hand to reveal an empty shell casing. "I found this, Lieutenant." Gasping like a race horse, Ja'meena looked at Esther with panicked eyes. "I also found moccasin prints. Oh, sweet Jesus, there's no telling who has taken her. Lieutenant, we have to give chase."

Garrett held the shell casing between his thumb and forefinger. He stiffened, his brows drawn together in a deep frown. "This must be from when Private Reece fired his rifle."

"B-but, we must search—" Ja'meena didn't get to finish her sentence.

His top lip lifted in disdain. He shouted, "Corporal Tibbets, are we ready to roll?"

Esther grabbed his arm. "No! We can't leave. You have to search for Birdie. She's out there somewhere. She might be hurt."

Whatever fragile lines of friendship had formed disappeared like a puff of wind. "My orders are to get you people to the depot and loaded on the train by day after tomorrow. As far as I'm concerned, Miss Dix is expendable."

Esther and Ja'meena joined forces. Ja'meena's eyes flashed fury. "Your fancy word is not lost on us, Lieutenant. Dare not forget that we are educated women. Just because we were taken captive and forced to live as less than humans does not mean we have lost our intelligence. Birdie's safety is your responsibility. You cannot leave her any more than you would leave one of your men."

Rage swept across his face. "I can...and I will." He snatched the leather gloves from his belt and proceeded to pull them on as he jumped from the wagon.

He barked out orders. "I'll drive the lead wagon. Tibbetts, wagon two. Smith, bring up the rear. Keep a steady pace. I intend to arrive in Livingston by nightfall."

"Sir, what about meals?"

"There's plenty of jerky, water, and hardtack in each wagon, Corporal. Fifteen-minute stops to rest and water the horses and for the people to take care of personal needs. Now let's get these wagons rolling."

****

The train whistle shrilled, while a puff of gray smoke billowed upward toward a mean sky. A scarecrow of a man dressed in a black suit and wearing a black-billed hat checked his gold watch and shouted, "'Board! Last call."

"This isn't right, Esther. The old ones and children loaded into a stock car as if they are no more than cattle." Ja'meena crossed her arms over her breasts.

"It is the way of things, Ja'meena. Even if we protested, our words would fall on deaf ears." Esther frowned. "Besides, it is time."

Ja'meena nodded. The two women hooked arms, determination in their steps as they approached Lieutenant Garrett.

He cocked an eyebrow. "Why aren't you aboard, ladies?"

"We're not going," their voices rang in unison.

He sputtered. "What do you mean...you're not going? I have orders—"

174

"We *know* your orders." Esther spat the words. "Your orders are to escort the people to Colville Reservation. Corporal Tibbets and Privates Smith and Reece are to return to Fort Ellis with the wagons."

Ja'meena tapped her foot impatiently. "Private Reece is a long way from healed. He can't drive, and you'd have to leave one of the wagons here, with its horses." She smirked. "Esther and I can both handle a team. We are your third drivers. When one of us gets tired, the other will take over."

Esther leaned forward, her face inches from his nose. "Like it or not, Lieutenant, we're free women who volunteered to go to Colville. Now we are *un*-volunteering because we intend to search for Birdie."

"And kill the bastard who took her," Ja'meena replied.

He held forth a brown folder and spoke evenly through gritted teeth. "Ladies, you are trying my patience. Your names are on this official document. You are now in the custody of the United States Government. I'm respectfully ordering you to get aboard the train."

"The government can't own us. We're not livestock, and certainly not slaves." Ja'meena's entire body jerked with anger.

Garrett blew out a disgusted sigh and rubbed his temple as if he were in pain. "Corporal Tibbetts, Private Smith, ready your arms. These women are under arrest. Put them on the train, and if they resist—shoot them."

The corporal stepped forward. His eyes contrite, he lowered his voice. "Sorry to do this. You're nice ladies, and I 'preciate what you done for Private Reece." He pointed his rifle. "I ain't never shot a woman before.

175

Please don't be my first."

Both women narrowed their gaze in silent reprimand. They gathered their skirts, hiked them above their knees, and climbed the two-rung metal ladder to disappear inside the boxcar.

Esther leaned out, her glare fixed on the lieutenant's frown. She called out, "You better hope that Birdie is alive and found unharmed. If not, I pray her spirit haunts your dreams for the rest of your life."

A railroad worker slid the massive wooden door closed and lowered the bar in place, locking the occupants away from the outside world.

Garrett scribbled a brief note and handed it to the corporal. "Wire this immediately to Colonel Culpepper." He snapped a salute. "Safe journey back to Fort Ellis."

The corporal returned the salute as his lieutenant bounded up the steps and disappeared inside a coach.

The conductor grabbed the railing of a Pullman coach and jumped aboard. The metal wheels turned in a slow, grinding complaint that grew to a clack becoming faster and louder as the engine picked up speed and rolled out of the station.

"What's it say, Tibbetts?" Private Smith peered over the corporal's shoulder.

"Lieutenant's writin' is worse than mine. But it says: One casualty. Private Reece knifed. Resting at hospital in Livingston. Miss Dix whereabouts unknown. Possible abduction. Due to schedule did not give chase. Nineteen bound for Colville. Detailed report later."

The private harrumphed. "We got time for a beer before we head on back, Tibbetts? I got me a powerful thirst."

Tibbetts pulled his coat tighter against the chill. "It's *Corporal* Tibbetts...Private Smith."

The train whistled a shrill final announcement of its departure as the two cavalrymen strolled toward a local saloon.

Chapter Twenty-Two

The last of October, an icy wind whipped around the column of troopers and the scraggly defeated band of Nez Perce. Travel had crawled over the miles at a snail's pace from Bear Paw Mountains to the outskirts of Livingston. The train depot was less than a half mile from General Miles' present location. The tops of buildings and the lights from a few gas lanterns were visible, as were the sounds of civilization.

Putrid odors wafted from A Company's ambulance, for lack of proper medical facilities for the wounded and those sick with influenza. Chief Joseph's people had taken turns riding in the short supply of wagons. Many had walked, the weak and wounded transported on horse-pulled travois.

General Miles raised his hand and signaled to halt. He gave the order to dismount and passed the word to set up camp.

Ford and his men had completed their mission. He looked forward to a few days off, a bath, shave, and a hearty meal before heading back to Fort Ellis. When he returned, he planned to do whatever it took to win Birdie's trust.

Sergeant Major Miller offered Ford a canteen. Ford noted the deep weariness in the sergeant's eyes and the droop of his shoulders. He gazed down the line and saw the same weariness in his men. They were bearded, dog-tired, and cold. If there were complaints, he knew the men were too exhausted to voice them.

He drew a long draught of stale water from the canteen. He swished the inside of his mouth and spat.

A corporal from A Troop approached. He offered a weary salute. "General Miles requests an audience, sir. His quarters are being set up yonder." The corporal pointed.

Ford nodded as he handed over the reins to his mount. "It's getting dark. See to the men and horses, Sergeant Major."

Ford turned away. He shook the ache from his shoulders, but the throbbing pain in his arm remained. By the time he arrived, the general was seated in his favorite fold-up chair, and a light glowed from a lantern.

"Let's dispense with the formalities, Captain." He motioned. "Sit." He handed Ford a shot of whiskey.

Ford thanked the officer. He remained silent.

"The Indian problems are over. Tomorrow, I and my lieutenant will ride into town to confirm the number of railcars needed. Once Joseph and his people are loaded, I'll relinquish official command of your troopers back to you. Whether you allow your men a short furlough in town or return immediately to Fort Ellis is your responsibility."

"Understood, sir. One request—permission to ride in with you tomorrow."

"Permission granted. Dismissed." Without a salute or further acknowledgment, General Miles stood and disappeared between the flaps of his tent.

The brusque dismissal rankled Ford. He was tired, the men and horses were exhausted, and the Nez Perce pushed beyond human limitation. He hadn't agreed with the general's treatment of the captives and had openly voiced his concerns.

He tossed the untouched whiskey to the ground.

Several hours later, two shadowy figures stood outside his tent. "Cap'n?"

A fire pit had been dug in the center of the tent, and flames flickered. Gradually life had returned to Ford's limbs. "Enter."

As Ansel and Isaiah entered, Ford motioned toward the pot of coffee. Ansel slapped his hands together. "Don't mind if we do, sir. It's colder'n the tits on a boar hog."

They laughed at the old joke.

Seated and their hands wrapped around tin mugs, no one spoke for a moment.

"What's on your minds?"

"Well, Cap'n, the men are wantin' to know if they can go into town tomorrow. It's been a long haul. They'd like to wet their whistles and take care of their pistols. If'n you know what I mean, sir." Ansel looked over at Isaiah and winked.

Ford grinned. "Our eighty plus General Miles' men equals to near one hundred fifty soldiers. I'm not sure the town is ready for such rowdiness." He steepled his fingers against his lips and released a heavy sigh. "In the morning, I'm riding in with the general to send a wire to Colonel Culpepper. Ansel, I'm leaving you in charge. Isaiah, hitch one of the wagons and follow me. We'll go to O'Shaughnessy's Tavern and purchase several kegs of beer and a case of whiskey. The men can drink their fill in camp. As for relieving their *pistols…*" He smirked. "I'll see if I can arrange for a couple of wagons of good-time dollies to visit before we head back to the fort."

Isaiah grinned. "The men'll like that, suh." He furrowed his forehead. "You reckon the ladies are still at the fort? I sho got me a hankerin' to see Miss Ja'meena. And suh, if'n she'll have me, I plan to put in fo' my retirement. I done give the Army forty years of my life, and I'm plum tuckered out."

Ansel nodded. "I've been thinkin' along the same lines, Isaiah." He tossed the dregs of coffee into the fire. Hot coals sizzled and ashes floated upward. "I'll relay the information to the men. 'Night, sir."

"Suh, I been seein' how you're favorin' that arm. Better let me take a look."

Without complaint Ford unbuttoned the long row down the front of his shirt. He flinched as Isaiah lifted the arm and unwound the bandage. "Shoo-wee, cap'n, I don't like the looks of this." The sergeant wrinkled his nose. "Don't smell right, neither. You bes' let me scrape out this yeller stuff, and—"

"I know, fill it full of turpentine." Ford huffed a painful chuckle.

"No, suh. I got some new stuff from General Miles' medic, called carbolic acid. Now, it's fo' sho gonna burn. The medic says it's good for killin' infection. And then he gave me some little white pills call aspirin to help with the healin'."

Leaning back in his chair, Ford met the sergeant's concerned gaze. "Do what you have to do, Isaiah, and get it over with."

The curly-headed sergeant lifted a brawny shoulder. "Jes' so you know...I take no delight in hurtin' you." He removed a broad-bladed knife from its sheath and held it over the flame.

Ford's heart thudded against the inner wall of his rib cage as Isaiah dragged the hot tip of the knife's blade along the inside of the wound, scraping out yellow pus until fresh red blood flowed. Then he filled the area with carbolic acid. Ford's harsh breathing was now reduced to raspy gasps.

Isaiah handed him two round white pills and a bottle of whiskey. He mauled a smile as he wrapped Ford's arm with a fresh bandage. "I'll sho 'nuf be glad when we get back to the fort, so you can have some real doctorin'."

"You did fine, Isaiah." Ford swallowed the pills. Ready to immerse himself in the bottle of whiskey, he stretched his long legs toward the fire's meager warmth.

****

Early the next morning, Ford stood on the dock watching the train disappear. He had about decided that everything was going to work out for the best. General Miles had seen to the care of his sick and wounded, Joseph and his people were on their way to Oklahoma, and once Miles had delivered them to the proper authorities, he and his troop would return to Fort Laramie for some well-earned rest and relaxation.

Meanwhile, Ford and his men would return to Fort Ellis, where life would continue until the next assignment. Isaiah's comments about marriage and retirement had beleaguered Ford's mind. Times were changing; the West was changing, leaving him unsettled about his own future desires. He rubbed the back of his neck wearily. A grayness overcame him, a mixture of exhaustion and powerful thirst.

A thirst for Birdie.

He wanted to hold her, to drown himself in her. To spend the rest of his life with her.

"Army sure is keeping the railroad busy. It hasn't been more than a week ago that we shipped a carload of Nez Perce to that reservation in Washington, somewhere near a place called Kettle Falls."

A short, smooth-skinned, pudgy, jowled face peered at him from under a red knit sweater cap. The man reminded Ford of a fat elf.

He frowned at the clerk standing next to him. "Are you sure?" he asked tersely.

"Sure as I'm standing here." The clerk held out a clipboard, his finger pointing to the date on the document. "It's plain as day. One rail car loaded with twenty Nez Perce departed Saturday, October twenty-seventh."

Closing his eyes and drawing in a deep breath, Ford said, "Did you observe three women who were not Indian?"

The squatty clerk scrunched his eyebrows together. "It was colder'n a jaybird's bare ass, Captain. Couldn't hardly tell who was who 'cause they all had blankets draped over their heads." He snapped his fingers. "Come to think of it, one woman's blanket slipped to her shoulders when she lent a hand to help an elderly woman climb up the ladder. I remember thinking that Indians had straight black hair and hers was…well…frizzy-like."

Ford's heart sank. "Ja'meena."

"What's that you say, Captain?"

"Their names? Do you have a list of their names?"

"Nah, only the number of poor souls being

183

loaded." The clerk tapped the clipboard with a pencil. "Twenty, to be exact."

"Did you, perhaps, see a woman with red hair and a scar that resembled an X?" Ford traced an X on his cheek.

"With the Indians?"

Ford's temper heated. He wanted to reach out, grab the clerk's shoulders and shake him until his eyes fell out. "Yes, with the Nez Perce, you fool. There were three women, two white and one black. Sending them to the reservations is a mistake. That's why it's important to know if you saw them."

The pudgy workman stepped back, his eyes wide. "I done told you, Captain, I didn't see any of their faces. If I had, I'd be telling you."

Ford blew a snort of vexation and left the depot, his long legs striding rapidly toward his horse. A feeling of dread swept over him. "Damn. Dammit to hell!"

He cantered down Main Street toward O'Shaughnessy's Tavern, then down a side alley and to the rear of the building, where he spotted Isaiah jumping from the wagon, a surprised look on his face. "Cap'n?"

A pensive sigh escaped Ford's lips before he realized he was as tense as a twisted cord. "Glad I found you, Isaiah. We have a situation. By sheer accident I've discovered that the captives from Fort Ellis are on their way to a reservation in Washington."

The first sergeant cast a doleful look toward his captain. "Lawdy, suh! What 'bout…"

"Them too." Ford muttered a curse in roweling frustration. No amount of wishing that the clerk had made a mistake would change the outcome. "Take the wagon and head on back to the camp. As soon as I arrange with O'Shaughnessy to haul out a brew wagon, I'll catch up with you."

"What 'bout the whores for the men, suh?"

Wearily Ford rubbed a hand across his face as he sought some practical solution between going after the women and satisfying his men. "Returning to Fort Ellis and obtaining permission from Colonel Culpepper to secure passage to Colville Reservation is more important than poking some harlot's honey hole for two minutes of pleasure."

A smile played at the corner of Isaiah's mouth. He nodded vigorously. "Yassuh, anythin' else?"

Ford cocked an eyebrow at the man. "I have a stout hunger for steak. Have the men ready a trench for barbequing thick steaks to go with their beer." He winked. "Poor substitute for nestling between a woman's legs, but it'll have to do."

Isaiah's chuckles flowed out behind him as he slapped the leather reins and gee'd up the mules. "Yassuh, I 'spect so."

Ford swung from the saddle. He tied his horse to a rail and mounted the steps that led to the tavern's back door.

With arrangements made, thirty minutes later Ford's heart lifted at his success as he reined his horse toward the encampment.

****

By midmorning, the exhilaration of last night's steaks and beer had worn off as the column of troopers rode toward Fort Ellis, their shoulders hunched against the cold. Ford found himself rubbing the back of his neck and realized a deeply seated ache had established itself there, no doubt from his own tension. As he rolled his head to ease the discomfort, his mind flittered to finding a reasonable explanation as to why Birdie and the other two women had been sent to a reservation. Had they gone of their own choosing? Or was Colonel Culpepper ordered to treat them as captives? No amount of rationalizing satisfied him.

A strange restlessness swept over him as he stared out over the landscape patched with snow. Although he couldn't exactly pinpoint what he craved, the feeling was nevertheless intense. Part of it, he determined, was the desire to recapture the contentment that had been his before the discovery of Birdie. He'd always considered the Army his home...his family. Yet whatever plagued him was infinitely more complicated than that.

He had been a bachelor too long, purposely avoiding serious relationships with marriage-minded women. In plain reality, he *needed* to be with Birdie. He couldn't bear the anguish of never seeing her again.

After a day of riding, Ford lifted his hand to call the column to dismiss and set up camp. As was his habit, he invited Ansel and Isaiah to join him for a nightcap.

Ansel swore under his breath. "I can't believe we missed them by two days."

Isaiah's lips were tight. "What I can't figure is why dey left the fort. I bet that Miz Ledbetter and her cacklin' hens had somethin' to do with it."

Ford finished off his brandy. It warmed him. His gaze dwelt absently on the mug in his hand. He looked up suddenly and felt a dart of elation that a falling man feels when his hands latch on to something solid. He cocked a grin. "We each have at least thirty or more days of accumulated leave time. Suddenly, I have a hankering to visit the great territory of Washington, and I can't think of better traveling companions than the two of you."

The idea grew quickly and became a plan.

****

On the third day out, the branches of pines were wrapped in fleecy banners of snow. The gelding's lazy pace lulled him. In his mind Ford saw Birdie lying still, asleep. He reached out to touch her shoulder, to enfold her in his arms. Her face was soft, her smile inviting. Her eyes were like twin emeralds flashing their lustrous green fire. It was a curious fantasy.

His horse snorted, breaking the reverie. Topping a rise, he drew rein. "We'll take a fifteen-minute breather, Sergeant Major. Pass the word."

"Wait! Belay that order." Ford stood in the stirrups. The sun had risen and was so bright he squinted to focus beyond the shadows of the pines. "Is that wagons?"

Ansel reached around and whipped the field glasses from his saddlebag. He held them to his eyes. An expletive exploded from his lips. "Hell and damnation. I'm damn sure that…it is, Cap'n." He handed the glasses to Ford. "They're wearing cavalry uniforms. Could be renegades dressed like soldiers. Reckon it's a trap of some sort?"

Ford shook off the remains of his daydream. "Give the order to double-time, Sergeant Major. Let's find out. Upon approach and with saddle guns ready, have the troop form a circle to detain the wagons."

He touched his heels to the gelding's flanks,

sending him forward.

At the sergeant major's command, a trooper galloped forward and grabbed the reins of a wagon horse. "Hold up there."

Ford, with rifle ready and followed by his sergeants, approached the lead wagon.

The tow-headed, freckle-faced corporal on the wagon's seat snatched off his hat. "D-don't shoot. It's me, Corporal Tibbitts and Private Smith." His tenuous grin grew from ear to ear. "Hot damn and twelve ways to Sunday, Captain Thackery, what are you doing here? We thought you were with General Miles."

Ford gave the order. "One hour, Sergeant Major."

Ansel bellowed, "Dismount! One hour for nooning."

Ford frowned at the two men. "Step down and join me." He lifted the flap on his saddlebag to remove an oilcloth. He unwrapped the cloth to expose several thick slices of jerky.

"Thank you, sir. We've got plenty." Tibbetts and Smith declined the offer. He followed the captain.

Ford removed his knife and sliced off a healthy piece of beef and placed it in his mouth. A breeze barely tickled the leaves on the cottonwood trees. He sat with his back against a tree and chewed thoughtfully as if he didn't have a care in the world. "Where is your commanding officer?"

Tibbetts and Smith sat cross-legged. It was Tibbets who said, "Lieutenant Garrett escorted the captives to Colville Reservation, sir."

Ford nodded thoughtfully. "Why didn't he come back with you?"

"Sir, on Colonel Culpepper's orders, the lieutenant

was to personally escort the captives to their destination."

A moment of silence followed. Ford noticed the slight tic at the corner of the corporal's mouth. Ford remained silent, letting the young non-commissioned officer sort out what was bothering him.

Ansel and Isaiah joined the small group.

It was almost as if Tibbetts couldn't stand up to his captain's icy stare. Finally, Ford said, "Do you know why Misses Dix, Bullard, and Pickett were sent to Colville?"

Tibbetts looked away for a moment. "No, sir, I don't." There was guilt in his face and his voice. Like a water main that had broken, Tibbetts related how Private Reece had been stabbed and Birdie kidnapped, and that because of the tight schedule to get the captives to the depot and aboard the train the lieutenant had said there was no time to search for her.

Tibbetts drew a breath and continued. "At the depot, Miss Bullard and Miss Pickett refused to get inside the boxcar. They wanted to travel back with Smith and me to search for Miss Dix."

Tibbetts stared down at his feet. He rubbed the back of his neck. "When the ladies refused to get aboard, the lieutenant placed them under arrest. He ordered Smith and me to shoot them if they tried to escape. He also ordered me to send a telegram to the colonel informing him that we'd had a casualty, and a possible kidnapping, although he didn't say it was Miss Dix."

Anger edged Ford's voice. "Let me get this straight: Lieutenant Garrett ordered you to *shoot* Miss Bullard and Miss Pickett if they didn't get aboard the train?"

Tibbetts opened his mouth several times but couldn't seem to get the words out.

"Dammit, Corporal, answer me!"

Tibbetts managed to croak out, "Yes, sir. Those were his orders. Private Smith will confirm."

Ford glanced down the line at the soldiers. He balled his hands into fists and worked to quell his anger. "How close are we to where the abduction took place?"

Tibbetts stood. He didn't hesitate when he pointed. "About two miles beyond that rise, sir, there's a grove of aspen trees. We camped there for shelter. That same night, Miss Bullard and Miss Pickett searched as best they could. They repeatedly called Miss Dix's name. If it hadn't been for a moon that night, I doubt Miss Pickett would have found the moccasin print." He shook his head. "What with the snow and the wind, there might not be any sign of the camp left."

Ford followed the direction of the corporal's arm. His jaw taut with anger, he kept his voice calm. "Other than the moccasin print, was there further evidence that Miss Dix was possibly abducted by a renegade?"

Tibbetts nodded gravely. "I can't say, sir. Our orders were to get the wagons ready to roll out on the half hour. We did as the lieutenant instructed."

Private Smith added, "Sir, we didn't hear anything. No scream or nothing, until Private Reece was able to fire a shot."

"Thank you for this information. I'll expect a detailed written report from you and Private Smith once we arrive at the fort." Ford offered a salute. "Dismissed."

Tibbetts and Smith returned the salute. "Yessir. Thank you, sir."

Ford's teeth ground together in vexation to think of what might have happened to Birdie. "Sergeant Major...First Sergeant?"

"Yahsuh?"

Ansel met Ford's grim expression. "What you got in mind, Cap'n?"

Ford turned crisply to face his troopers. His voice lifted sharply. "Men, I'm placing Sergeant Major Miller and First Sergeant Bohanan in charge while I pursue the criminal who abducted Miss Dix while she was in the protection of Lieutenant Garrett."

Without a flicker or a twitch of the lip, he said, "First Sergeant, I'll need an extra horse and provisions."

"Right away, suh." Isaiah pointed to a trooper. He barked. "Unsaddle your mount and hand over the reins. Then go to the mess wagon and gather up 'nuf food to last the cap'n fo' a few days. Yo' can ride to the fort in one of the wagons."

Tension grew in Ford as he shook hands with the two men he trusted the most. "See to it that both Tibbetts and Smith file their reports. Better still, read over the reports to make sure no details were conveniently left out to protect Lieutenant Garrett. Also, let the colonel know that if I haven't returned in a week I'm either dead or still searching for Birdie and the fiend that kidnapped her."

He swung into the saddle. Almost as if reading their thoughts, he said, "Give me a week before you decide to go after Esther and Ja'meena. Depending on what shape she's in when I find her, I'm certain Birdie will insist on going with you."

Ansel and Isaiah stood back, clicked the heels of their boots together, and snapped off a salute.

Shaking off unpleasant thoughts, Ford rode east to locate the cold camp where Birdie was last seen.

Chapter Twenty-Three

Birdie roused. Night had fallen. The last thing she remembered was slumping forward, her arms draped on either side of the pinto's neck. She was stiff and sore, and so completely exhausted that she was unable to distinguish between tensed muscles and utter fatigue. She was also very thirsty. The granite walls and the rocky soil were barren of snow. She tried to push thoughts of food from her mind; nevertheless, she wondered how long she could go without proper nourishment.

She remembered offering up a prayer to the Great Spirit Father to guide the horse out of the arroyo. Just how far she had progressed through this difficult maze was a mystery. Looking up at the sky, she searched until she turned the horse in the direction of the North Star. As the pony plodded, and the night wore on, it was becoming more and more difficult to keep from sliding out of the saddle. She would feel herself slipping, would be about to fall, and then somehow manage at the last instant to wrap her hands around the saddle horn and haul herself back into position. The saddle had become increasing uncomfortable, chafing her inner thighs. She tried to stuff her chemise and skirt underneath her to protect her vulnerable areas.

Birdie knew Indian ponies were famous for their unpredictable temperament. Whether it was from weariness or cantankerousness, the shift in her movement sent the pinto to bucking and crow-hopping in a circle, sending Birdie sailing out of the saddle. Stars glittered in front of her eyes as she rolled and her head bounced against a boulder.

She lay on the cold ground until her vision cleared. Her fingertips came away wet when she touched the back of her head. She hoped the gash wasn't serious. Pushing to a sitting position, she considered staying right where she sat, for it would only cause her more pain to move. Laughter bubbled out of her—an eerie sound in the barren wilderness. She had survived starvation, unmerciful beatings, rape, and kidnapping. She thought it hilarious that she would die because she was lost and couldn't figure out how to unlock the puzzle to find an opening in the numerous mazes. But hunger and thirst were very strong incentives to keep moving. Wincing, she managed to push to her feet. In the midst of her despair, a soft nicker drew her eyes to the pinto.

"You sorry bag of bones," she railed, her voice a woeful lament. "Throw me again and I'll feed you to the vultures." Birdie was certain she was becoming addled, threatening the horse. At this point she didn't really care.

Treading lightly, she approached the gelding and grabbed the one dangling rein. Carefully setting her foot into the stirrup and easing into the saddle, she waited for an interminable length of time before she touched a heel to the gelding's flanks. Reassured that he wasn't about to repeat his earlier performance, she turned him in what she fervently prayed was the right direction. They walked for a lengthy bit of time before

Birdie allowed herself to slightly relax. Still, she wasn't of a mind to trust the pinto and kept a tenacious grip on the saddle horn.

After plodding over the treacherous terrain for untold hours, Birdie was grateful for the luxury of riding rather than walking.

The breeze that had sprung up earlier had strengthened, bringing with it a damp chill which did nothing to bolster Birdie's spirits. Earlier she'd had hopes of surviving this horrendous situation. Her heart sank and new fears congealed in her chest. A snowflake landed on her forehead, and then two. A moment later a wet snow began pelting her.

She groaned in despair as she dug her heels into the gelding's flanks. The horse didn't rebel. Instead, he quickened his pace, but the wet stony ground caused him to slip and stumble, hampering his progress.

The falling snow thickened into a dense white curtain. Birdie could barely see, much less move any measurable distance. In only a few moments her clothes became thoroughly drenched, until the moisture had seeped all the way through her coat to her chemise.

In spite of the chills wracking her body, she had one positive thought—at least now she had all the water she could drink, if she didn't freeze to death first.

The gelding, anxious to escape the icy flurries, surged forward, only to lose his footing and fall to his knees. Birdie clung to the saddle horn to keep from flying over his head. The poor animal struggled to right himself. Unable to believe that the Great Spirit ill-favored her by allowing these circumstances, she fought the urge to sob. Again she reminded herself that Indian women didn't cry. Chagrined, she looked up at the dark

gloom and spread her arms wide. She screamed,
"I…am…not…Indian!"

The pinto shivered. She felt him hunch and waited
for the buck. "Easy, boy, steady," Birdie murmured
through fear-stiffened lips. "It's okay. We're okay.
We're alive. At least for the moment."

She reached forward to pat the dripping wet
brown-and-white neck. The horse calmed a bit but
stood shivering.

In growing panic, Birdie glanced about, hoping to
spot some way of escape. The horse's fatigue was
becoming apparent. Blinking through the sodden
tendrils of hair that streamed down her face, she
dismounted and proceeded to lead the pinto. The
headstrong horse shook his head, planted his feet and
balked. Tenaciously, Birdie gave several sharp tugs,
pleading with the animal to cooperate. "Listen, you
stupid son of a burro, I'm trying to save your life, and
mine, too. So move!"

The horse stepped gingerly forward. She cajoled,
"That's it, boy. C'mon, you can do it."

As if understanding the logic, the horse surged
forward, bumping against Birdie's shoulder and
propelling her backward. To her horror water splashed
over her head. Birdie sensed her impending doom.

****

Ford touched spurs to the gelding's flanks, urging
him forward to where he hoped to find evidence that
would lead him to Birdie. Thoughts played cat-and-
mouse games with his mind. Why didn't Lieutenant
Garrett immediately send a trooper to the fort
requesting aid to search for Birdie? Why didn't he send
Corporal Tibbetts ahead to escort the people to the

depot while he stayed behind to search for Birdie? Why didn't the lieutenant send his wounded trooper along with Esther and Ja'meena back to Fort Ellis?

A strong tide of revulsion and anger continued to rage inside him as he considered different avenues to punish the lieutenant. First and foremost was standing Garrett in front of a firing squad for dereliction of duty, or perhaps a court martial and loss of retirement. Ford decided that option wouldn't wash because Garrett was obeying the colonel's orders to get the people to the depot on time.

For whatever reason, bias must have colored Garrett's decision not to search for Birdie, but what rankled him just as much was ordering Esther and Ja'meena to be shot if they didn't join the others inside a cattle car. A *cattle car!* As if they were no better than animals.

Ford shook his head and muttered a curse. Once he returned to the fort and had an opportunity to read over Tibbetts' and Smith's reports, he would recommend that Garrett be stripped of his rank and sentenced to six months in the brig. That was, if Colonel Culpepper didn't take action first.

Eventually Ford spotted the grove of aspen trees and rode toward it. He dismounted and secured the horses. He untied a bag of oats from his saddle and fed each gelding a meager handful; then he set about searching for clues.

He cut a stout branch and used it as a probe to sweep back and forth through the dirty slush. He was about to return to the horses when he spotted a blackened, jagged tip poking through the snow. Using the toe of his boot he cleared an area that revealed the remains of a campfire. He squatted. A week had passed, and the ground beneath the muddied ashes and burnt sticks was stone cold.

He lingered over the spent fire pit for a long moment. His breath clouded the air, and he wondered if the sun would eventually break through and drive the chill away. Calling on the skills that Levi High Eagle had taught him, Ford figured that due to the inclement weather the campfire would have been built close to the wagon. Squatting on his haunches, he goose-walked to where he imagined the rear of the wagon sat. He crouched low, and using both hands smoothed away the snow. A strange elation built in his chest. His eyes marked two, deep, water-filled ruts. Only a heavily loaded wagon would leave such an imprint. He allowed a small satisfied smile to tug at the corners of his lips.

He searched until he located three more dead campfires and sets of muddied wagon ruts. With hands on hips, he now knew which had been the lead wagon and the last wagon. He surmised that the lieutenant would drive the lead team, and going on gut instinct, Ford figured that wagon would include Birdie.

He stepped over the ruts and measured off a distance that Birdie might have walked to take care of her personal needs. He figured about sixty paces. She knew better than to stray too far in the dark. They were in mountain lion country, and half-starved cats were unpredictable.

The distance led him into a thick carpet of the aspen grove. Snow hung like dew drops from spiny tree limbs, and beams of sun haloed through the dense grove. He squatted and with meticulous care brushed away small patches of snow. A half hour of searching for clues that indicated Birdie had been abducted at this spot left him disappointed.

His legs had grown numb and, as he struggled to stand, felt like thousands of needles prinked his skin. He stamped his feet to awaken the blood flow and to lessen the pain. A long wavering sigh escaped his lips, leaving his spirits deflated.

He was losing daylight, and hunger and frustration gnawed at his belly. Trying to decide whether to take time for a short meal or push on, he turned. A slight movement in the brush caught his eye. There it was. Right in front of him and he'd almost missed it.

As if he were plucking a delicate flower from its stem, he untangled the strip of brown and orange tweed. Victory bubbled inside his chest. This piece of cloth had been ripped from the ugliest coat ever—Birdie's coat.

He rubbed his aching arm. He was fevered, and he knew it. He removed two more of the pills from the box Isaiah had given him and allowed them to dissolve on his tongue. A meager smile tugged on his lips as he uncorked the bottle of brandy and tossed back a draught. He was tempted to draw a second mouthful. Instead, he placed the flask back inside his coat pocket. He gazed out over the tree-studded grove. Night came early in November. A few stars began to twinkle through the leafy shroud as his thoughts wandered back over the conversation with Corporal Tibbetts. Anger riffled through him as he imagined Birdie's fear. He yearned to find her, to comfort her.

Wearily, he rubbed his hands over his face. He was fatigued and rationalized that it was better to postpone his search; it was no use trying to track in the dark.

Chapter Twenty-Four

The gelding's ears pricked. White puffs of air formed as the horse blew and snorted. Ford shifted the snow-crusted brim of his hat farther away from his brow, fully alert that the horse had heard, sensed, or seen something. Ford peered through the flurry of flakes and the dreary grayness of the early morning.

He twisted in the saddle, glancing in every direction. He saw nothing of importance. He removed his field glasses from the saddlebag and levered them to his eyes, slowly perusing the landscape. Reaching down, he stroked the gelding's sodden neck, regretting that he didn't have his own trusty warhorse, which was recuperating back at the fort. "What's out there, boy? What's spooked you?"

The horse nickered and pawed the ground. Ford tilted his head, listening intently. He could hear little against the constant sifting of snow against the ground, the slight creak of his saddle, and the shifting of his mount.

He cuffed a hand against his ear, hoping to muffle the extraneous sounds. And then he heard it—the gurgling of a stream and the distant shrill whinnies of a horse. He touched his spurs to the gelding's flanks, sending him forward toward what he truly hoped was the area from which the sounds seemed to emanate. His own gelding stretched its long neck and answered the whinny. As Ford drew closer, he grew certain that what he was hearing was the shrill whinnies of a horse and not the wind. If that were true, he prayed he'd also found Birdie.

Following the urgent shrieks, Ford reined his gelding through the trees and over unpredictable snow-covered terrain. When he broke through a tangle of woods into a clearing from whence the piercing whinnies came, what he spotted in the distance sent his heart into spiraling alarm. A brown-and-white pinto stood at the edge of a stream attached to some type of tether. Ford's gaze followed the length of leather stretched tight between the horse and a...body. His breath left him in a rush when he spotted the red hair. Birdie lay half in and half out of the icy water, her arm stretched upward with one single rein wrapped around her wrist and gripped tightly in her fist.

"Birdie!"

Ford spurred his mount into a gallop and then hauled him to a skidding halt. Wasting no time, he swung from the saddle. The pinto's hair-raising scream increased Ford's foreboding. The animal pawed and splashed with one hoof. Ford's boots slipped and slid on the icy ground as he sprinted forward, keeping his voice calm as he spoke to soothe the frightened animal.

At the edge of the stream, Ford unsheathed his knife and cut loose the rein gripped in Birdie's hand.

Red heat fired through him. Someone had battered her beautiful face almost beyond recognition. One eye was swollen shut. He wasn't sure if her lips were purple from the cold or from the deep cuts. A gash above her swollen eye needed stitching.

He lifted her into his arms, out of the water, and

laid her gently on the ground before he rushed back to aid the pinto. As he grabbed the other dangling leather strap, he saw its leg was solidly wedged between two boulders, and the animal shivered from exhaustion and cold.

Talking and rubbing a reassuring hand down the pinto's neck, Ford planted his boot against the smallest of the stones and used all his strength to shift it enough to free the horse's leg. For a moment it seemed his efforts were futile. Then, the horse lunged forward, nearly jerking the rein from Ford's hand.

The instant the pinto realized he was free, he whinnied in triumph and tried to flee. Ford gripped the bridle's cheek strap. Muttering an oath, he spotted the coyote symbol on the stirrup's fender: the symbol of a cunning trickster. This was Levi High Eagle's horse.

He had never shot a man in cold blood. For High Eagle he'd make an exception. "Damn you! I don't know if you're alive or dead, but I'm making it damned hard for you to survive and get help." Ford drew his knife, reached under the horse's belly, and ripped through the girth, rendering the saddle useless. He yanked the saddle from the pinto's back and dropped it to the ground, keeping hold of the blanket.

He yanked the bridle over the horse's head and cut the bit from the cheek straps, then tossed the mouthpiece into the stream. With a stinging smack to the rump, he sent the horse flying, its tail flagged in freedom.

A strange blend of fear, shame, and relief swept over Ford as he knelt and wrapped the blanket around Birdie's sodden body. Until he could get her back to last night's campsite and build a fire, the warmth from the pinto's blanket would help stem the chattering of her teeth.

Muttering an oath, Ford scooped Birdie into his arms, carried her back to his horse, and lifted her into the saddle. Swinging up behind her, he clamped a protective arm around her and reined the gelding toward the dense aspen grove where he'd left the spare cavalry mount tied.

At last night's campsite, he crafted a rough lean-to shelter from fir and aspen branches. Spacious enough for two people and a small fire pit, the temporary refuge would serve them until Birdie was able to travel. He set about building a fire to heat water, coaxing enough warmth to chase the chills away from both of their bodies.

His lean fingers worked the sopping wet coat from her shoulders. He worked his way down her torn, filthy gown. She lay deathly still as he slid it down her body, pulling away both her chemise and pantalets. He removed her shoes and stripped away her stockings.

When she was completely nude, he looked at her a long moment. She lay on a bed of fir needles covered with his tarpaulin to hold out the ground's moisture.

In the flickering firelight, her soft breasts glowed like two luscious golden orbs. Though he yearned to taste their sweetness, he refused to lower himself to further strip Birdie of her dignity. He knelt on his knees and watched her for a mere second. Such sights were too much of a temptation. He turned aside and grabbed his saddlebag to pull out a pair of woolen socks and a clean shirt. For the time being his garments would provide her with a little warmth.

His eyes flicked down her naked body again as he

slid her arms into the sleeves of the shirt. The garment all but swallowed her and reached to her ankles. He lifted one leg and pulled a sock over her foot and rolled it up to her knees. His fingers itched to explore further.

He finally lent his attention to the matter of food. He set about slicing bits of beef jerky into two cups of water. Although he had plenty of canned provisions, and cold corn dodgers, without knowing how long Birdie had been without food he didn't want to overload her stomach and add retching to her malaise.

****

She did not want to wake up. It was the large hands removing her wet clothing that startled a fearful gasp from her. She forced her eyes to open. A man hovered over her. He was hardly more than an ominous gray shadow inside a crude shelter, and she thought his eyes glowed with a feral light. In her delirium and thinking he was Levi High Eagle, she shrank back and had some difficulty breathing as she awaited her fate. Drawing up in a small, disconcerted knot, she waited to be punished.

The snow had seemingly spent its furor. Birdie was thoroughly depleted, both physically and mentally. Though she tried to remain alert, her eyelids sagged beneath the weight of her fatigue. She tried to lift her head, until a large hand pressed it down gently against a sturdy shoulder. Her brow found a warm niche for nestling, against a corded neck, and with a sigh, she gave up her futile attempts to remain conscious. If Levi High Eagle intended to kill her, he would have done so by now.

Darkness had fallen. Birdie roused briefly to a vague awareness that the snow had ended. A cold, blustery wind had sprung up. The frigid breezes evoked shivers. Birdie reached to tighten her coat closer to her body, only to realize that she wore strange clothing. A hairy arm drew her snug against a bare chest. She found no energy to resist but nestled closer to soak up the warmth. As she drifted off to sleep again, she was reminded that once again she had been captured and wondered distantly if she would ever find a safe haven.

Once, in rising fear, she struggled against him and thrust her hands against his chest. Then, with a muted sob, she collapsed in a fit of coughing. Though she allowed him to draw her back within his encompassing arms, in a few moments he felt her stiffen again. Her head thrashed against his shoulder, and when he tried to shush and soothe her, she gave a sudden wail and strained away from him as if he had become the devil himself. But when she began to mutter in her sleep, he realized she was locked in whatever nightmarish cruelty Levi High Eagle had thrust upon her.

It was much later when Birdie struggled up from her dazed trauma and realized that it was Ford who sat cross-legged feeding a fire. Smoke curled invitingly from a circular pit with a soft glow from the flickering flames.

A croupy cough rattled out of her throat, causing Ford to turn. Feeling suddenly wary, she drew back. Hesitantly, she met his gaze and saw a handsome brow twist upward.

"Captain Thackery?"

Noting her bewilderment, Ford smiled. "Hungry?"

"Starving."

He offered her a tin cup. "Careful. It's hot."

She almost drooled over the bubbling liquid. "I

can't remember the last time I've eaten."

Ford's warning came too late. Eager to fill her belly, Birdie drew a mouthful of hot beverage which scalded all the way down to her belly. She coughed, her eyes watered, and her nose dripped. She found the flavor well worth the pain. Blowing before taking another cautious sip, she made small noises of appreciation and then greedily finishing the remains in the cup.

She licked her lips. "What is it?"

"Bits of beef jerky and boiling water." He used his knife to poke around in the ashes and gently edged a round metal pot toward him. He used the tip of the blade to lift the lid. "I hope you like day-old corn fritters."

Birdie's eyes lifted to his smiling face as he handed her a fritter. She took a bite, savoring it to the same degree as the broth. "You should eat, too." She pressed her fingers against her lips and licked away the spots of grease as she chewed.

She followed his progress as he broke off a piece of bread and plopped it into his mouth. He chewed thoughtfully. "Coffee should be ready. Hold out your cup."

As he busied himself pouring the coffee and handing her another fritter, she eyed him with careful diligence. His sun-bronzed face seemed to glow against the firelight, highlighting his dark chestnut hair and the expanse of his broad shoulders. As he leaned across the fire pit, he seemed to loom over her in a manly magnificence.

Birdie shrank back, troubled by the feelings he awoke within her even in the face of her cruel treatment by Levi High Eagle. A feeling of anxiety plagued her. "High Eagle…he's coming. I can feel him."

She closed her eyes and lay back on the canvas blanket. Hot and cold chills set her teeth to chattering. A ragged cough tried to suck her breath away. Ford scooted to her side. He touched his hand to her forehead. Her skin was cold and clammy, yet her luminous green eyes glowed with fever.

She grabbed his hand and met his gaze, recognizing an unspoken query in his blue eyes. Talking exhausted her. "I stabbed him…in…" She tried to smother another cough. "Stabbed…in the arm…and then…I stole his horse…and—" Her breast heaved as she labored to breathe.

****

Ford reached up to test the articles of clothing he'd hung over the fire. Much to his chagrin, her shoes and socks and other garments were as wet as when he undressed her. He had no idea how long she had lain half submerged in the icy stream, but he was fair certain that from the chills and fever and chronic cough she was well on her way to having pneumonia. A feeling of dread swept over him; without proper medicine, she would die.

He wanted to protect her—felt an urgent need to protect her. He prayed the wind would settle its vicious lashing of the trees. Somewhere in the distance, a coyote yodeled. Birdie's eyes flew wide, and an indistinct murmur passed from her lips. She thrashed about, throwing the blanket to one side.

His arm ached. The stench of infection offended his nostrils; his own fever had returned. In the morning, come what may, they would leave this place. If he didn't get her to the fort soon, they both might die.

He opened the flask of brandy and touched the opening to Birdie's mouth. He urged her to take a sip. "It will quiet your cough. In the morning we'll ride for Fort Ellis."

She opened her one good eye. "How far?"

"Three days. Maybe two. I have an extra horse, so we can push hard."

"The pinto?"

"No. A cavalry mount."

She reached up and touched his face as if she were seeking his strength and whispered, "Ford, kiss me the way you did the day we went riding."

Mindful of her bruised and swollen lips, his mouth came down on hers softly and tenderly. She closed her eyes and, in a hushed voice, he thought he heard her say, "Thank you."

Chapter Twenty-Five

Startled out of a sound sleep, Ford reached for his revolver, his body shocked awake as if someone had doused him with a bucket of ice water. Levi High Eagle knocked the crude lean-to aside, his left arm bound up in a poorly created makeshift sling and a pistol gripped in his right hand.

"Drop it, Captain, or I'll put a hole in the bitch's head." High Eagle lowered the sights on Birdie.

"High Eagle!" Ford roared.

Birdie sat up clutching the blanket to her chin, her eyes riveted on the smug face of her abductor. She lowered her eyes to the revolver.

"I'm putting it down," Ford stated as he took great care to place the revolver in full sight. "Now turn your weapon away from Miss Dix."

High Eagle's yellowed teeth gnashed in a pain-filled grimace as he reached to grab Ford's weapon and tucked it inside his waistband. Lifting crazed eyes to meet Ford's, he rasped through his agony, "That damned, ungrateful wench tried to cut my arm off. When I come to, she'd stolen my horse."

He pointed to the flask. "Open it. Don't try jumpin' me, 'cause killin' you won't bother me."

Ford obeyed. High Eagle thumbed back the trigger of his pistol. "I'm takin' a swig. Don't be a hero, Captain."

High Eagle lifted the flask to his lips and emptied the contents, then threw the bottle aside. Grimacing, he spoke through his pain. "Lucky for Woman with Iron Fist that she escaped, 'cause when I come to, I was in a mind to cut her into little pieces for leaving me with a useless arm."

His bellow wrenched a start from Birdie. He jeered, "Before this night is over, I'll have me some of that you're tryin' to hide, Woman with Iron Fist."

Birdie struggled to keep her expression passive as she sidled next to Ford. Apparently, he wasn't as shaken as she was. He said, "There, inside my saddlebag, is a bottle of whiskey. It's yours if you can get it without hurting your arm."

High Eagle harrumphed. "You think I'm falling for that trick? I'm not a stupid Indian, Captain."

"Okay, then tell me—how did you get out of the guardhouse?"

"I was let out on good behavior, maybe?" High Eagle snarled savagely. "I escaped, you dumb bastard."

Ford rose to one knee. "It's obvious you're in pain. Let me get the whiskey for you."

High Eagle staggered. A sheen of sweat glistened on his brow. He raised the pistol. "Nah-uh. Stay where you are."

In a bold move, the Pawnee reached out and grabbed Birdie's wrist and jerked her forward. "If you want to save your captain's life, you will come with me and beg to live."

Birdie let out a yelp as she tried to jerk free, but his massive hand had clamped around her arm.

Ford roared like a wounded bear as he staggered to his feet and bolted forward, grabbing the weapon.

Birdie slumped forward, prickled by the cold feeling of death.

High Eagle lashed out with his foot. He yelped in pain as Ford landed a vicious punch to the wounded arm. Locked in a macabre dance, the two men wrestled for control of the gun. Ford felt his own injured arm weakening as he strived for more strength.

Birdie struggled to sit upright. Unable to tear her eyes away from the battle, she flinched when Ford stumbled.

The explosion echoed through the stillness. Steel blue smoke curled upward between the two men's bodies. Locked together, both men dropped to their knees.

"Noooo!" Birdie screamed, grabbing High Eagle's good arm. Surprise flickered across his face. The gaping hole in his chest sucked in air as he struggled to draw a breath.

She trembled at his sullen expression. "Start diggin' his grave." Red spittle dribbled down his chin, and he slewed to one side.

She grabbed Ford's shoulders. "Ford...Ford, are you shot?"

Ford blew out a long laborious sigh. He clutched his injured arm. "No."

A scarlet stream stained the sleeve of his jacket. He swayed, nearly dropping to his knees.

The rise and fall of Birdie's chest was alarmingly shallow as she hastened to his side. She strained to bear his weight. "Let us leave this place—now."

Through heavy-lidded eyes, he looked at her. "I love you, Birdie. If I die, let my family know where I'm buried."

She answered in a broken voice, her eyes filled with tears, "You are a mighty warrior, Captain Thackery. Warriors continue to fight even as they are gasping their last breath."

Ford nodded, his silence telling her he understood.

While he saddled the horse, Birdie labored to stretch the dead Pawnee onto his back. She placed two stones from the fire pit to hold his eyes shut. "Your soul cannot meet the Great Spirit Father." She spat on the twisted face. "He would not want you anyhow."

****

Wrapped in the pinto's horse blanket and wearing Ford's rain slicker, she hunched in the saddle while Ford used the old Indian technique of tying the spare horse to the tail of his gelding. She opened her mouth to speak but a coughing spasm replaced the words.

Ford swung up behind her. Shifting his hat forward over his brow, he wrapped his arms tight around Birdie, pulling her close to his chest.

The wind had blown itself out. The sky had cleared from a gunmetal gray to an inky black littered with stars.

The gelding behind them nickered its impatience. Ford gigged his mount forward, setting a course for Fort Ellis. For several miles he held his horse to an easy lope, until Birdie's fever burned against his chest and her limp body put a strain on his arms.

He pushed the horse into a gallop. Riding double, he figured if they rode steadily they could cover about forty miles by sunup.

They rode for a long time in silence. Birdie's head alternated between bobbling against his chest and lolling forward. He rolled his shoulders as the land stretched out before him. Layers of pink and purple colored the sky as the sun sank in the west. Then shadows began to creep from rocks and brush, and soon they were surrounded by darkness.

Birdie's question came on a heaving gasp. "How much farther do we have to go?"

"Two days."

"Please, we have to stop. My body hurts all over."

His first impulse was to stay the course. Common sense ruled. He reined the bay gelding. "We'll camp over there for the night. I know this place." In the scant light, he pointed to a screen of scrub brush. "There's a hollow in the rocks beyond those bushes with room for the horses. We can sleep for the night and they can graze without our fearing they'll wander off."

Birdie shivered as she heaved a raspy sigh. "Maybe the rocks held some of the day's sun and we can warm up a bit."

Ford dismounted. He reached up to help Birdie from the saddle. "I'll take care of the horses and set up camp while you take care of your personal needs."

He drew the revolver from the holster at his side. "Take this with you. It's better to err on the side of caution."

Not understanding his meaning, she cast him a puzzled look.

Ford quirked a smile. "Never mind. Just keep the revolver handy."

When she returned, a fire was burning. He had opened a can of beans, and coffee was perking. "My mouth is hungry, my stomach not so much. If it's not much trouble, I would like jerky broth." She handed him the revolver and sat down, her back against a large, warm boulder. "I want you to know that I'm grateful to you for saving me from Mud Pony. The one you knew as Levi High Eagle."

His dark eyes expressed the grief he felt. "I'm sorry he hurt you."

She touched the tender areas on her face. "No matter. He is dead."

His eyes flicked up at her remark.

"Why did they leave me…Lieutenant Garrett…I mean? I could hear Esther and Ja'meena calling my name. Mud Pony stuffed a gag in my mouth. I could not answer." She shrugged an indifferent shoulder. Life had taught her that whatever happened was beyond her control to change; she must accept the consequences.

Ford rolled his tired shoulders. "There is no excuse for the lieutenant's actions other than that he was under direct orders to get the captives to the train and on their way to the reservation. He considered his first obligation was to Colonel Culpepper's instructions."

Birdie did not make an attempt to bridle her words. She lifted a quivering chin, bestowing a glare toward him. "Humph! Just like any warrior. Getting rid of the enemy is more important. What was one less person to care about?"

Ford swept her a lengthy perusal before straightening uneasily. He handed her a cup of jerky broth and a cup of coffee. She drank ravenously, and so did he. Then he left to take care of his personal needs. When he returned, Birdie had curled into a ball, her hands folded beneath a cheek. She tried to dream of Ford…but disturbing dreams kept getting in the way.

****

Ford truly wished he had a bottle of whiskey. He

didn't know which hurt the most, his arm or Birdie's testament of Garrett's not bothering to look for her. Garrett's actions toward Esther and Ja'meena certainly implied a certain prejudice. The man had shown unmistakable disrespect and lack of good judgment.

Lifting his cup, he silently toasted Birdie. She was quite a woman. He wiped the cup clean and set it upside down on the heated stones. Treading quietly, he looked down at Birdie's sleeping figure in the dappled light. It was much like considering a lavish feast and not knowing where to begin.

Bending a knee, he leaned down until he lay braced on an elbow next to Birdie. It took all his will power to resist the temptation to touch her, only admire her dainty features and softly parted lips. Looking at her awakened his male urges, which had gone unappeased for too long. He feathered a kiss on her cheek. *You've made me crave everything about you.*

He wrinkled his nose. The foul odor on her breath possibly meant that her lungs were filled with infection. He tucked the blanket tighter around her shoulders. Gathering her in his arms, he pulled the tarpaulin over both of them. Tomorrow he would push the horses harder.

Chapter Twenty-Six

Birdie's first thought upon awaking was that she had been deserted. Ford was nowhere to be seen. A fire flickered in the fire pit. The coffeepot sat on a heating stone. The spare horse was still tethered nearby, but not the bay gelding. In an instant, she felt more helpless than when she had escaped Levi High Eagle. Glancing around, she had no idea where she was.

Snowy wilderness stretched on for miles. A dazzling blue sky usually meant a warm day. The early morning chill suggested otherwise. They had been traveling due east. If she could manage the strength to get on the pony, she would follow the same course, all the while fearing she would succumb to exhaustion and faint, only this time there might not be anyone to find her before the vultures did. There was enough snow to quench her thirst. She would think about food later.

"G'morning." His voice startled her.

"I thought…never mind. Where were you?"

"We're out of jerky. The corn fritters are all gone. I was out scouting for berries. Didn't find any." He shrugged. "The only thing left is a can of beans."

She coughed until her head ached. Reclining against the boulder, she said, "I am not hungry."

He handed her a cup of coffee. "Try to drink this. You need something to keep up your strength."

She lifted the cup to her mouth, but her stomach

rebelled. She closed her eyes to rest a moment more before another day's long ride. She looked forward to visiting with Nora. Most of all, she longed for a hot bath and food that didn't make her sick. She wondered if Elmira Ledbetter and her group of witches would still treat her like poison. The few weeks she had been away from the fort seemed like a lifetime. Were Esther and Ja'meena happy at the reservation? Would she ever see them again?

Ford reached out to press cool fingertips against her forehead, then drew back, concern lining his face. She tried to smile. She wanted him to pull her against him and feel his lips on hers while his hands caressed her all over.

"Birdie...Birdie?"

His voice cut into her thoughts, and she came crashing back to reality to realize she had broken out in a feverish chill. Her breath came in labored gasps, and for a moment she couldn't speak.

"What?"

Doggedly, he said, "If I have to run both horses into the ground, I'm getting you to the fort by nightfall." Getting her to a doctor was all that mattered now, making sure she was safe.

He emptied the remaining coffee into the fire. Using his boot, he scattered the hot ashes. His movements quickened as he saddled the bay and tied the spare horse to the gelding's tail.

He lifted Birdie into his arms and raced to the bay horse. Her limp dead weight made it difficult for him to hoist her into the saddle.

She looked at him through fever-glazed eyes. "Untie the horse. We will make better time."

"No, Birdie. We need him."

"The Comanche know that a pony will follow its leader. He will follow. Trust me."

They rode into the day, Birdie sitting in front of him as he held her tightly, and the spare horse trailing behind.

"Hold on, Birdie. Don't leave me," Ford whispered.

Placing her hand against her breast, she was stunned to feel the warmth radiating. Ford was thinking of her. Her heart actually burned with the intensity of the love that enveloped her. In that moment, as the sun rose in the clear blue sky, Birdie knew she had found what she had spent a lifetime searching for. Not her dead mother's name or her brother who had disappeared at age two. Not freedom from being a captive slave. It was called happiness, happiness with a man who loved her—not for breeding purposes but because she was simply—Birdie.

Indeed, she had found it, but now that she was dying, did she dare reach for it?

And was she willing to fight to hang on?

She felt herself slipping…slipping into a dark void. It felt as if night had wrapped about her. It was hard to see anything. Where was Ford?

Don't let it be too late, she prayed, every nerve screaming as desperation surged. She called out to him, the sound echoing forlornly in the darkness…

Finally, surrounded by emptiness, she knew it was hopeless.

Chapter Twenty-Seven

The November cold grew, wrapping itself greedily around Ford. The need of sleep was telling on him. The morning hours ground away. Fire burned in his stomach from tension and sleeplessness. The steady riding was wearing him down. In spite of the cold, he sleeved sweat from his face. Weakness assailed his body. He thought if he could have a little something to eat it might help.

Birdie cried out, "Ashkii."

In her delirium she mumbled her son's name and spoke in words that Ford didn't fully understand. Here and there he recognized a Pawnee word or a Cheyenne phrase. Other times she whimpered.

Once, in apparent fear, she roused enough to struggle against his arms. Then, with a muted sob, she had collapsed against his chest.

The bay gelding quivered, its breathing labored. Ford knew he'd pushed the horse to exhaustion. He needed to stop, to change mounts. He feared that once he assisted Birdie to the ground, caught the other horse, and saddled it, that he might not have enough energy to lift her back to the saddle.

Every muscle, every bone in his body ached. For Birdie's sake he would call on whatever reserves of energy he had left. Easing the lathered gelding to a stop, Ford leaned Birdie forward over the saddle horn and supported her with one hand while he dismounted.

It took a moment to steady his legs. He grabbed Birdie around the waist and eased her to the ground. She lay still—so very still that he knelt and placed his cheek against her lips. Barely a breath, but it was enough. "Hang on, my brave girl. We're almost to the fort."

The bay gelding hung its head, body quivering, sides heaving. Ford removed the bridle and stroked the weary animal's neck. "You deserve a medal and additional oats for going the extra mile. You're a damned good cavalry mount."

Fresh and feeling frisky from the weather, the young sorrel played a *catch me if you can* game with Ford. He loosed a string of curses, calling the spare horse every name in the book. Every time Ford approached, the sorrel squealed, backed away, or hiked its tail and pranced just out of hand's reach. Without a lariat, it was impossible to rope the animal. Aggravated, Ford decided to take a breather.

He sat on the ground next to Birdie. He scooped a handful of snow and rubbed it over his face. The chill provided the desired bracing effect. He filled his mouth with icy crystals and allowed them to melt down his throat. His taste buds desired a hot cup of coffee.

Struggling to his feet, Ford draped the bridle over his shoulder and walked toward the sorrel gelding. He offered the palm of his hand, allowing the horse to inch closer before he reached out to grab the halter's cheek strap. Unlike the more seasoned cavalry horses, who stood patiently, this wall-eyed sorrel reared back, jerking free of Ford's grip.

Ford cursed the fleeing animal. He pulled his

revolver, aimed, then holstered the weapon. "Why waste a bullet?"

He looked soberly at the bay. The animal was too spent and probably didn't have a half mile left in him.

Ford slung the snow-filled canteen's strap crossways over his shoulder. He hefted Birdie into his arms. His footsteps crunched in the snow as he set out for the fort. His right leg slipped, and he stumbled under the weight. He didn't know how long or how far he'd walked when he paused to catch his breath in the icy air. Near exhaustion, he collapsed to his knees.

As he rested, he retraced the tedious journey that had brought him to this point. "We're going to make it, Birdie." Was he reassuring her or himself? He chuckled at the thought.

The hollows in her cheeks seemed to have deepened. They had both grown awfully thin.

Ford struggled to his feet with Birdie slumped over his shoulder. He managed to stand straight, although weakness pulled at his knees. He had walked a couple hundred yards when he thought he heard the jingle of wagon traces. He stopped and cocked an ear, certain it was only the wind. Five minutes later, he was convinced he was delusional. He had read about French Legionnaires lost in the Sahara Desert who'd seen mirages of oases and had died filling their bellies with sand, all the while thinking it was water.

"Cap'n…Cap'n Thackery."

Ford laughed aloud. "You hear the wind, Birdie. It's playing tricks by calling my name."

Hardly daring to believe what his eyes told him was true, he watched the wagon draw closer. He spied a black soldier standing, legs braced apart. A stockier trooper held tight to the wagon seat.

Damned if he wasn't seeing a mirage right here on the Montana prairie. Isaiah drew back a whip and cracked it over the team's head. Ford laughed again. It came to him that he had cheated death for the last time.

****

First Sergeant Isaiah Bohanan hauled back on the reins and set the wagon's brake. Sergeant Major Ansel Miller jumped to the ground, and Isaiah followed. Both men grabbed Ford and Birdie, bracing them before their captain wilted to the ground.

"Yo' jes' hold on, suh, whilst we get you and Miss Birdie in the wagon."

Ansel tucked blankets around the shivering couple. He uncorked a bottle of whiskey and touched it to Ford's lips. "Just a sip to warm you up, sir."

Ford choked on the swallow. He gasped out, "Birdie... Is she alive?"

Isaiah propped Birdie against the side of the wagon. He gently pinched her cheeks together to force her lips open. "C'mon now, for ole Isaiah...it ain't the bes'-tastin' whisky, but it'll..." The amber liquid dribbled down her chin. Her eyes remained closed. "Sergeant Major, we better get these hosses hightailin' it back to the fort. She's in a mighty bad way."

Ford wrapped his hand around Birdie's. He drew in a weary breath. "How'd you know to look for us, Isaiah?"

Isaiah chuckled. "That mule-headed sorrel gelding that none of the troopers like to ride...well...danged if it didn't come runnin' into the fort early this mornin' like his tail was on fire."

"Yessir," Ansel cut in, "we figured it'd broke loose

and left you afoot. We knew the other horse might've played out, so Isaiah and I told the colonel, and we set out. We were already getting worried 'bout you."

"Mighty proud to see you. Don't know how much longer I could have kept going." Ford stopped talking. He ran his tongue over dry, wind-burned lips. He raised his head. "How far?"

"'Bout five miles….Hold tight, suh. It's goin' to be a bumpy ride." Isaiah snapped the whip. He hi-yupped the team. The buckboard lifted on two wheels as he spun the horses around and toward the fort.

****

Sometime later, Birdie became vaguely aware that someone was carrying her through a dark area. She heard the sound of a door closing, and then muted voices seemed to drift upward as if from a deep well. A glowing lamp moved somewhere beyond her, casting elongated shafts of light on the walls and ceiling. A door's hinges creaked as it opened and then closed. She barely remembered being placed upon a bed. She tried to wake when she heard Ford's concerned voice. But a woman's tones banished him from the room.

Gentle hands lifted the man's Army blouse over her head and drew her arms from the sleeves, a blanket draped over her nude body. The movements seemed obscure and distant, as if she only dreamed them. She felt a warm wet cloth on her face and more warm moisture moving up and down her arms and legs…her entire body. And at long last, she felt a nightgown being drawn over her head, down her shoulders and arms, and then a blanket being tucked in around her.

A strong arm lifted her…a man's arm…not Ford's. A woman's voice encouraged her to open her mouth. A spoon touched her lips, and warm liquid, the most delicious broth she'd ever tasted, slid down her throat. She wanted to open her eyes, but the lids refused.

Then a lantern at the end of a long tunnel was snuffed, and darkness closed in around her as she sank deeper into a dreamy void and had no desire to awake.

Chapter Twenty-Eight

Ford dozed in his big chair, his stockinged feet stretched to garner the potbellied stove's heat. His hand rested on the book in his lap. Somewhere between dreamland and wakefulness his thoughts strayed between tumbling horses, violins, and screaming painted faces.

Barely had he nodded off than a light rapping sounded on the door of his private quarters. His eyes popped open and he rolled them around in their sockets until he brought the room into focus.

The rap came again, this time a little louder. "Captain Thackery, I have the folder you requested. You've also got mail and a package."

Another voice intruded, loud and gruff. "Listen, you young dunderhead, don't be disturbin' the cap'n. What with all he's been through, he needs more'n two days to recuperate before you go botherin' him."

"B-but sir, I have the file he requested, and a stack of mail. One letter looks important."

"Go on back to pushin' your pencil, Private. I'll deliver it."

Ford tried to sort out the voices in his fumbling, sleep-dulled brain. He croaked a response, massaging his throbbing temples. "Enter, Sergeant Major."

"Hold the door wide, Sergeant Major. I've brought the captain lunch." Nora Culpepper bustled through the

225

portal. She ordered, "Pull the table closer to his chair."

Ansel Miller obeyed. Nora relieved herself of the tray. She swept back the towel that covered the dishes. "Chicken noodle soup, fresh baked bread, a slice of pound cake, and a pot of coffee." She scolded, "The soup is nice and hot. Don't let it get cold."

Hands on hips, she glared a warning at the sergeant major. "See to it that he doesn't leave a drop in the bowl." And then she waggled a good-natured finger. "There's plenty of coffee. Now don't you go helping yourself to the cake, Ansel Miller."

The sergeant major reached out and opened the door for Nora. He offered a sheepish grin. "Yes, ma'am, thank you, ma'am."

Ford sat up, setting the book aside. His stomach rumbled as he inhaled the soup's savory aroma. "Help yourself to the coffee." He cocked a lopsided grin. "There's enough cake for both of us."

Ansel smacked his hands together. He drew up a chair. He handed the manila folder and stack of letters to Ford. "Thoughtful of you, Cap'n."

"Have you read the reports?"

Ansel washed down a forkful of cake with a sip of coffee. "Yessir. Pretty much on point. Neither Corporal Tibbetts or Private Smith skirted around Lieutenant Garrett's actions."

"Has Colonel Culpepper seen the statements?" Ford savored a spoonful of soup.

Ansel brushed cake crumbs from his shirt. He leaned forward and lowered his voice. "Ah, not before I read 'em first." He winked. "All I can say is I wouldn't want to be in the lieutenant's boots."

Neither man spoke for a moment. Ansel seemed

distraught when he spoke. "I peeked in on Miss Birdie." He shook his head. "We never did trust Levi High Eagle, did we, sir?" The question bore no response. "If ever a man needed killin', it was him. 'Specially with his ill intentions toward Miss Birdie."

Ansel released his breath a second time. "Before I leave, I thought you'd like to know that after the colonel read the report, he immediately sent a telegram to the agent at Colville reservation instructing him that Esther and Ja'meena were to return to Fort Ellis pronto, and the lieutenant, too. Well, that wasn't his exact word."

Ford looked up at the grinning sergeant. "What else, Ansel? You're grinning like a canary that ate the cat."

"The stage is due to arrive around noon tomorrow. I surely hope seeing her friends will be the strong dose of medicine Miss Birdie needs to put roses back in her cheeks."

In spite of the throbbing in his head, Ford managed a smile. "Doc Pope said he's surprised she's alive. While he and Nora were washing Birdie's hair and combing all the burrs and critters out of it, he found a quarter-size gouge in the back of her head. On top of the severe beating and the pneumonia, he's certain she also suffered a concussion."

Ansel tsked as he rocked back on his heels. He seemed a bit discomfited. "Now, this ain't going to come as no surprise to you, Cap'n, but just so you know, Isaiah and me...well...we've put in our papers for retirement. The official forms will go out in tomorrow's mail when the stage arrives, but to speed things up, Colonel Culpepper sent a wire to the

Department of the Army Headquarters in D.C. He said we should get confirmation in about thirty days, more or less."

He continued rocking back and forth. "And...uh...you see, sir..." He drew a deep breath and let it out on a gasp. "We plan to do some serious courtin' when the ladies get settled. We're hopin' to wed before we leave the fort."

Ford and Ansel both stared at each other. Ford said, "Where will you go?"

"I'm from Mississippi and Isaiah is from Georgia. Both places have seen too much war. We agreed on North Carolina. We'd have the mountains, flat land, and the ocean. We plan to build separate houses with porches for rockin' chairs and facin' the ocean, not too far apart, so the wives can visit."

Looking a bit sheepish about sharing his future plans, Ansel said, "You're lookin' a little peak-ed, sir. Didn't mean to wear you out." He opened the door. "If you need anythin' I'll come a-runnin'.""

Ford tossed a grin toward the sergeant major. "It's good to have a plan. Just don't forget to give the women a say-so in those ideas."

Alone, Ford leaned back and closed his eyes. Realizing his headache had ceased, he decided to read the report later. He'd already made up his mind as to the recommendation for Lieutenant Garrett's punishment. He flipped through the envelopes. He lifted a lilac-perfumed envelope to his nose. Pricilla Avery's name elicited a frown. He shuffled it to the back of the stack. Two letters demanded his attention: one from a boyhood friend, now the governor of New Jersey, and another, marked *Urgent*, bearing his brother's name in the return address.

Fearing the worst, he decided the letter from his brother needed full attention. He set it aside and opened the missive from New Jersey. The corners of his eyes crinkled into a smile. The contents of the letter contained more than he dared hope for. Carefully tucking the document into its envelope, he laid it on the table to share with Birdie later in the day.

He ran the blade of his knife along the gray envelope's spine, eager to read the other letter. He unfolded the sheet, at first scanning the page, then going back and giving full attention to his brother's neatly penned message.

Dearest Brother,

I will forego the usual salutations and come to the point. We need you home! Pop has met with a tragic accident. He was working a new thoroughbred stallion when someone left a stall door open. Jubilee escaped and immediately jumped the corral fence and attacked. Pop was caught between the two stallions and stomped in the head before one of the hands could get him out from under the tangle of hooves.

At this juncture Pop's thinking ability is about the level of a young child. The doctor doesn't give us much hope. Mother is beside herself. Dodson is on his way home from the Cape to supervise fall apple picking. He can't stay long because the ship-building business is thriving, and grandfather is too old to run it alone. I have been appointed to Congress and must leave for D.C. in a few days. James can't get home until Christmas. He's nearing final exams, and you know how rigorous the courses are at Oxford. That leaves you, Ford.

This is highly confidential, and it's my ace in the hole to convince you to put in for retirement immediately. With Chief Joseph and his band in Oklahoma, Geronimo in Florida, and the Cheyenne and Sioux defeated, the days of the Indian wars are over. The President is calling for closure of many frontier outposts. Fort Ellis is number ten on the list. There will be a mass reduction in military personnel. Most will either lose their retirement or have a severe reduction in pension. As I said, this is top secret and will not be announced until just before the list of fort closures is made available.

Further, all promotions in rank are currently suspended, indefinitely. I don't suppose I have to spell it for you. Before any of this goes into effect, put in for your retirement immediately and come home, Ford.

Your loving brother,

Robert

Everything went still. Reading about his father damaged something inside Ford. How long had it been since his last visit…five years…longer? He remembered his father as a vibrant man who loved his sons and adored his wife, brilliant minded, a man before his time.

He scanned the page and reread the words…*thinking ability is about the level of a young child.* My God, he thought, Father hasn't yet reached his sixtieth birthday. How could this be?

Cold shivers attacked. He needed warmth and stalked to the woodbin, adding several sticks of kindling to the potbellied stove. He moved his chair closer and pulled the lap blanket up to his chest. *All promotions in rank indefinitely suspended.* He didn't care about another stripe. It was the principle that annoyed him. Men in his command had died and lay buried in forsaken places; men like the sergeant major and first sergeant deserved to earn another stripe and a boost in pay.

He snorted a small laugh as he visualized the framed needlepoint that hung in his Grandmother Dodson's living room: *Family First.*

Decision made.

****

Birdie came awake with a start, not entirely sure why she had been snatched so abruptly from her dream. She lay for a moment trying to discern what was wrong, all her senses keenly attuned to the sounds outside the room. Beset with a chill and shaking uncontrollably, she searched down the length of the bed, patting her hands over the rumpled covers as she tried to find another blanket.

She remembered little of the past few days. Actually, she wasn't sure she was alive, though she reassessed her mortality when she tried to move and pain wracked her body. She opened and closed her eyes several times, hoping to sharpen her vision and determine where she was. The room seemed strangely familiar. She wondered what had happened and who had brought her to this place.

When at long last her vision cleared, she surveyed her surroundings. This was not the covered wagon she had shared with Esther and Ja'meena, and it wasn't the cave where Levi High Eagle had taken her. "Ford?" She thought she had spoken his name, but no sound left her mouth. She attempted to speak his name again. "Ford?" Still no sound. She balled her fists in frustration.

Hunger cramped her stomach; surely that was a good sign of recovery. She ran her tongue over her parched lips. She was also very thirsty. Struggling to lift on an elbow, she spotted a pitcher on a table. If she could just muster the energy to get out of bed and walk across the room...

A stout, gray-headed woman entered the room. Birdie gave her a timid glance. When the woman approached the bed and bent over her, Birdie favored her with a tiny smile. "Nora?"

"Birdie...bless be...you're awake. I'll get Captain Thackery."

"I'm a little thirsty. Could I have some water?" Birdie scooted against the bed's headboard.

"Of course." Nora poured a glass. "Do you need help, dear?"

"I'll help her, Nora."

Ford knelt by the bed. With concern darkening his face, his fingertips brushed across Birdie's pale cheeks.

She drank deeply of his strong, masculine features, and her thirst disappeared. She needed...wanted... nothing but Ford. He was all the nourishment she needed. In his arms, her body would heal.

He didn't speak...could not speak. Rather, his arms circled her shoulders and drew her up close to his chest, tears sheening his eyes.

Chapter Twenty-Nine

Birdie's stunning jade gaze turned up to hold his own. For the first time in her life she felt a sense of belonging. How happy she was, tucked beneath Ford's protective arm, his cheek resting ever so gently against her deep russet hair, and his rhythmic breathing in chorus with her own.

"I have a surprise for you." Ford lowered Birdie against the bed's headboard. He reached into his pocket to hand her the envelope.

Giving him a quizzical look, she unfolded the paper. The words on the page meant nothing to her. "It must be of some importance. What is it?"

"You remember telling me you were from New Jersey, correct?"

She nodded.

Ford took the letter. "I wrote to a friend in New Jersey, a man of importance, asking him to find information about Thomas Dix."

Birdie's body felt limp as damp weeds. "You found something about my family...my mother's name?"

He grinned boyishly. "Your father, Thomas Aslin Dix, was thirty-three years old when they left New Jersey in 1859. He worked in a foundry. Your brother was Thomas Aslin Dix, Junior, and your mother was Eliza Mae Birdwell Dix. She was twenty-eight years old. They joined the John Gannett wagon train with

Horace Reddeford as the wagon master. The rest you know."

He reached up to catch a tear on the tip of his finger. "I didn't mean to make you sad."

Birdie caught his hand. "These are happy tears. I am someone now, instead of *ohanzee*, a shadow." She repeated her mother's name, "Eliza Mae Birdwell Dix." She sighed. "It is a beautiful name."

"I have another surprise. Are you up to it?"

She drew fisted hands to her chest. Her smile widened. "There's more?"

The rumble of wagon wheels and a gruff masculine voice yelling, "Whoa!" interrupted Birdie's moment of elation.

"What is that commotion?"

Ford came fluidly to his feet. "It's the stagecoach. Bringing your next surprise, I hope." Beaming, he said, "I'll return in an instant."

Birdie tamped down her curiosity and waited.

In a moment, the infirmary door opened, and two smartly but simply dressed women entered the room, followed by Ansel Miller and Isaiah Bohanan.

Birdie squealed their names. "Esther…Ja'meena… my sisters!"

Amid the happy reunion, Nora arrived with a tray of lemon cookies and a pot of coffee.

****

Fifteen days after her rescue, Dr. Pope released Birdie from the infirmary with the admonishment that she was to get plenty of rest, plenty of sunshine, and to not overly exert herself.

The first morning's walk had evolved into a daily event, something Birdie loved and Ford encouraged—

and that she was receptive to his attentions pleased him very much. He had grown to love this courageous, soft-spoken, kindhearted woman so much he was certain his heart would explode.

Today he ventured to take her into his arms and kiss her. He was surprised that she showed little hesitancy; she was, after all, still wary of his intentions.

"What are you thinking, Ford?"

His hands spanning her tiny waist, her arms around his neck, he met her quizzical gaze in the soft light next to the river behind the fort. "I'm thinking that I never thought it possible that a woman like you existed."

"But…" She looked out at the mountains. "Elmira Ledbetter said you love Priscilla Avery, and that as soon as she returns to the fort, you will wed her."

Ford huffed a disgusted snort. "Priscilla is never coming back to the fort. She got herself in the family way, and her parents sent her East to live with an aunt."

Birdie's eyes widened. She tried to back away from Ford. "You?"

He replied truthfully, "No, Birdie. Never me!"

She did not smile. "Then Elmira Ledbetter is still a wicked woman."

Ford led Birdie to a patch of sunshine. His tone serious, he told her, "You are gentle and goodhearted. You are the kind of woman a man hopes for when he's ready to settle down. Be my wife, Birdie. Marry me."

Birdie extracted herself from his embrace, turning to face the mountains.

In a matter of moments, his hand fell gently to her shoulder, coaxing her back to him. "Did I say something wrong, Birdie?"

"No, Ford, you say all the things a woman desires

to hear. I simply am..." She shrugged. "I'm not sure you should say them to me when I'm..." She shivered. "Please, let's go back. I'm suddenly very tired."

He clasped her hands and kissed the knuckles. "I didn't mean to make you feel uncomfortable, Birdie."

****

She had been so lonely. She hadn't been with a man since shortly after the birth of her son. Moisture gathered on her lower lashes. She did love Ford, very much. The deep yearning within her for intimacy was almost too painful to bear. She wanted from this tall, quiet-spoken man what she had never known from any of the men who had pawed and slobbered over her and abused her body. She wanted love. She wanted to feel the warm and tender awakening of feelings too long suppressed.

A little voice inside her head said, *You do not run away from the man you love.* Her fingers traced the brutal scar that marred her face, a constant ugly reminder of her past life. Nausea stirred in the pit of her stomach. The need to get the words out was suddenly a compulsion.

Her breathing was dangerously erratic. "Ford... please do not interrupt until I finish speaking."

He met her gaze, a concerned frown pressed upon his brow.

Drawing in her bottom lip to cease her trembling, she reminded herself that she was not a coward. "Except for my son, and until I met you, I have never known the love a woman desires from a man. Now my heart flows like a waterfall with this emotion."

Her voice fell to a whisper. "You are a good, brave, honest, educated gentleman, and it is because of this that I will not marry you."

"Birdie…"

She held up her hand to stop him. "Please, let me finish. I speak Pawnee and Nez Perce better than I speak the language of my dead parents. I struggle to remember the words in English. Except for my name, I cannot yet write or read well.

"Don't you see, wherever I go, it will always be the same…I am a dirty squaw who should have killed herself instead of returning to live among *civilized* people. Wherever we go there will always be people like Elmira Ledbetter.

"You are an important man…" She fumbled for the words. "After a while, I would become an embarrassment and you would come to hate me."

Her eyes filled with tears and her voice hitched as she continued, "I could not bear your hatred. It is for these reasons I will not marry you."

Feeling as though her feet were mired in quicksand, she turned to flee.

Ford gathered Birdie into his arms as if wanting to absorb her mental pain into his own body. His chin nestled atop her red hair. "You are the most amazing woman I have ever known."

He explained about the letter from his brother and the condition of his father, and that he'd applied for retirement, with his plans to return home to run the family farm. "My mother is the most non-judgmental, caring woman you'd ever want to know. She and my brothers' wives will love you just as I do."

A knot formed in her throat when he said, "I want to live with you always, to watch our sons and daughters grow up, and you are so very wrong if you think I'd ever tire of you. Come with me, Birdie. My family's farm is a beautiful slice of heaven. We raise thoroughbred horses and have the best apple orchards in all of upstate New York."

She stood away from him to trail a tender finger down his face. She took deep breaths, wanting for once in her life to have something go right. Her hands cupped his face. Eyes locked with his, she whispered, "Ask me again."

Ford bent on one knee, he held both her hands, and smiled into her eyes. "Birdie Mae Dix, will you do me the great honor of becoming Mrs. Martin Ford Thackery?"

Tension she hadn't been aware of left her body. Her last fear had disappeared. Tears blurred her vision, and if she wasn't mistaken, tears swam in the deep pools of Ford's blue eyes. In a voice quiet with conviction, she accepted his proposal with another promise. "I will love you forever and always."

Chapter Thirty

The following Saturday morning was an auspicious day, sunny with clear skies, a day perfect for not one wedding but three.

Isaiah grinned from ear to ear as he led Ja'meena down the aisle of the fort's chapel, followed by a smiling Ansel with Esther's hand in the crook of his elbow, and then Ford touched Birdie's lips with a light kiss as he escorted her to stand at the altar facing the chaplain. Each woman was gowned in a cream-colored wedding dress.

Nora stood as the matron of honor and General Culpepper as best man.

****

It seemed scarcely a moment had passed before he was easing her onto the bed with its oversize quilt and fat pillows. When she sat up and started to untie the ribbons of her chemise, his hand closed over hers, halting their movements. "Don't...I would like to do that myself."

Her mouth molded into a seductive smile. Her palms flat upon the bed, her knees drawn up, she watched him as he undressed—the broad expanse of his chest with its thick mat of black hair, his slim waist and narrow hips...the full, male part of him that would soon join to her...the slim, muscular columns of his legs. When her eyes lifted to his own smiling ones, she knew he was very aware that he pleased her.

As she held his gaze, transfixed, his knee fell to the bed. With one foot still on the planked floor, his fingers moved to deftly undo her chemise. When at last his hands eased beneath the fabric to expose her shoulders, she shivered as the rush of cold brushed across her bare skin. Then his hands cupped her firm, small breasts, and his mouth lowered to capture one pink rosebud. Easing her to her back, her proud, impassioned cavalry captain covered her slim body.

When Birdie cupped his face between her palms, he lowered his lips to capture her parted ones, his hands gently kneading her breasts. His mouth hot against her own, his body so enflamed, she almost felt the surrender of her own flesh. Her hands went to the back of his neck to hold him close. His torrid possession scorched her like a brand, and when his hands slipped between her legs, coaxing them apart, her hips rose so that the hardness of him pressed against her. Before he could position himself to enter her, her hand lowered to gently guide him. Her boldness brought a twinkle to his eyes, and a moan escaped her as the utter pleasure of him deep inside enveloped her.

His hips began to move, slowly at first, then quicker, urging her to meet his masterful pace and blend into the exquisite blanket of sweet torment with him. Birdie thought she heard thunder, or did it come from within her own body?

Ford plunged deeper and deeper still, and she matched his rhythm and pace. Her skin flamed with a primitive desire that again tore a moan from her throat. In that moment, she sought his kiss and dragged her hands roughly down his shoulders to hold him close.

Then it came, the explosion deep within her that momentarily drove away the frenzied thumping of her own heartbeat.

When he was able to regain physical control, he lifted his head. "I didn't hurt you, did I?"

Still heady with passion, she thought how much she loved this man. She giggled, the happiness she felt vibrating in her voice. "No, but I am certain that in the fall we just might have our firstborn."

He hugged her close. "We're going to have a wonderful, exciting life, Birdie Mae. How many little Thackerys do we plan to have?"

Together they joked about twins, and how the boys would be a handful just like their...mother.

"Again, Ford. Make love to me again."

That evening as Birdie lay in her new husband's arms, she couldn't imagine being happier than she was at this moment. The weddings had gone off without a hitch, and even Elmira and her bevy of prune-faced followers had kept quiet and seemed to enjoy the small banquet Nora had prepared for them afterward. Birdie had no doubts that Ford was going to be a wonderful husband and a joy to be around for the rest of her life. She felt special, like a woman with the whole world at her feet.

Loretta C. Rogers

Epilogue

Sunday afternoon, Birdie sat at her desk in the second-story room that Ford had converted to an office. The journal Nora Culpepper had given her so many years ago lay open. Inside, Nora had written: *You survived what most women can never imagine. Tell your story, Birdie, because you have made history.*

Boyish merriment drew Birdie to the window. She opened the portal, allowing September's breeze to billow the white lace curtains. Below, her three sons and Isaiah's son playing stickball brought a tender smile to her lips.

She swept her gaze across the yard. Isaiah sat on the porch in his favorite rocking chair. His snow-white hair didn't belie his age. As foreman of Thackery Thoroughbreds, Isaiah was a genuine horse whisperer, as Ford never hesitated to brag.

Much to their chagrin, Ja'meena gave the boys piano lessons every Thursday.

Ansel's love of the soil and all things growing, plus always being the sergeant major, he supervised the farm's six apple orchards. When he wasn't working, he spent time teaching his godsons how to whittle. Esther's love of flowers and herbs had all their yards bursting with color. Never having had children of her own, she doted on Ford, Jr., the twins Huck and Henry, and Isaiah's son, Obie.

When he wasn't fishing, riding horses, or sailing on Lake Erie with the children, Ford spent time at the winery, perfecting different flavors of apple wine.

She had a full life…a happy life.

She stared out at the orchard a long time…on guard…watchful. She reached up and touched the scar on her cheek, tracing the puckered ridge down to the collar of her dress.

Ten years had passed since Ford and his troopers had rescued her and the starving band of Nez Perce. Ten years since he had saved her from the clutches of Levi High Eagle, and more than twenty years since the Pawnee had abducted her.

Two thousand miles lay between Montana and New York. With Ford, Ansel, and Isaiah, she was safe. Yet there were times when the moon cast dark shadows among the apple trees and amongst the horses in the corral that made her…afraid.

Caught in old memories that came flooding back to haunt her, she hadn't heard Ford when he entered the room. She flinched when he put his arms around her and rested his hands on her protruding belly. "Did I frighten you?"

She turned in his arms and rested her head against his chest. "It's September, and I was thinking about that bitter autumn so many years ago."

Ford tightened his arms, hugging her close. His chin rested on the top of her red hair. "It was my good fortune to find you." He glanced over at the desk. "Have you thought of a title for your biography?"

She shrugged. "Hmm. After discussing it with Esther and Ja'meena, I'm going to title it *Sisters by Circumstance*. They are as much of the story as I."

Ford nodded his approval as he swept his gaze down the length of her. Though she wore a charming dark green frock, it was obvious that she was with child. Birdie placed his hands on the round bulge to feel his child moving within her womb. "Esther says this one is a girl. I'd like to name her Eliza Ruth after both our mothers."

Ford kissed her neck. And then lower. "It's a beautiful name."

She caught her breath as his hands cupped her derriere, bringing her closer. Rather than respond with words, her hips rose so that the hardness of him pressed against her.

"Christmas."

"What?" Ford hesitated to release her.

She laughed against his mouth. "Our daughter will be a Christmas baby."

His lips touched her forehead in the gentlest of kisses. Birdie smiled to herself. With all its twists and turns, life was beautiful.

Birdie Mae's
Upside-Down Berry Cornmeal Birthday Cake

Because sugar was not readily available and therefore used sparingly during the frontier days, this cake is not particularly sweet, although it is easy to make and quite delicious. You can substitute your favorite berry: strawberry or blackberry, etc. If fresh berries aren't available, frozen berries work just as well.

Ingredients:

2 1/2 cups fresh blackberries (if using frozen berries make sure to thaw)

1 1/3 cups all-purpose flour

½ cup yellow cornmeal

2 teaspoons baking powder

¼ teaspoon salt

1 tablespoon basil (fresh-chopped or dry)

2 eggs, lightly beaten

½ cup sugar

2/3 cup whole milk **see note

1/3 cup canola oil

Container of Cool Whip (optional)

Garnish with fresh basil and/or mint (optional)

Directions:

Preheat oven to 350 degrees F. Lightly grease an 8-inch round cake pan. Line bottom of pan with parchment paper. Grease parchment paper. Arrange 1-1/2 cups berries in bottom of pan.

In bowl, stir together flour, cornmeal, basil, baking powder, and salt.

In separate bowl, whisk together eggs, sugar, milk, and oil. Add egg mixture all at once to flour mixture. Stir until combined. Pour over berries. Spread evenly.

Bake 40 to 45 minutes or until pick inserted near

center comes out clean.

Cool cake in pan 5 minutes. Run a knife around edge of the pan to loosen sides. Invert on a serving plate. Remove parchment.

To serve: top with Cool Whip and remaining berries, fresh basil or mint. Makes 10 servings.

Note: Almond milk or coconut milk may be substituted. Be aware that substituting either of these milks may significantly change the cake's texture and taste.

Saving Leftovers: If you're like most families you can't eat an entire cake before it gets stale. Of course, you don't want to throw it away. Here is my tip for saving leftover cake for later:

Slice cake into individual slices.

Set each slice on a sheet pan.

Place sheet pan in the freezer compartment of your refrigerator.

When slices are frozen, remove and individually wrap in plastic wrap or place in individual plastic sandwich bags.

Return packages of cake to the freezer.

To enjoy: unwrap and allow to thaw or place in a microwave for 30 seconds or in a toaster oven long enough to thaw. (You may wish to toast it spread with butter.)

Enjoy with your favorite hot or cold beverage.

Also from Award-Winning Author
Loretta C. Rogers…

THE WITCHING MOON
You Can't Hide from Your Past

Sheen O'Reilly considers her gift of second sight a curse. Branded as a witch, she wears a rope burn around her neck as a reminder of what happens to people who are considered different. Now settled in a remote homestead where she tends her animals and concocts herbal remedies, she knows "he" is coming but is powerless to stop him.

"He" is Guthrie Tanner, who blames himself for the murder of his wife and the kidnapping of his young daughter. After an unsuccessful year of tracking his enemies, he has heard about a witch who lives alone on the prairie. While he doesn't believe in supernatural nonsense, he is willing to do whatever it takes to find his daughter. What he doesn't count on is the effect Sheen will have on his heart.

Available now wherever books are sold.

A word about the author...

A native Floridian and proud of her Scots-Irish heritage, Loretta C. Rogers is a bestselling author. She writes in all sub-genres of romance. There is always a little bit of mystery and suspense in her novels. Her books are in libraries throughout the USA and Europe.

When not writing, she is an avid traveler, and enjoys researching her family genealogy.

HAPPY!

Your review is highly appreciated
if you enjoyed reading Bitter Autumn.

Visit Loretta at:

www.lorettacrogersnovels.com

Thank you for purchasing
this publication of The Wild Rose Press, Inc.

For questions or more information
contact us at
info@thewildrosepress.com.

The Wild Rose Press, Inc.
www.thewildrosepress.com

www.ingramcontent.com/pod-product-compliance
Lightning Source LLC
Chambersburg PA
CBHW060542260626
47161CB00003B/1011

* 9 7 8 1 5 0 9 2 3 1 2 4 9 *